ONE

THE TRILOGY OF WISHBONE HOLLOW

LAST

A NOVEL OF HISTORICAL FICTION

BORN

JOANN KLUSMEYER

Published by Innovo Publishing, LLC
www.innovopublishing.com
1-888-546-2111

Providing Full-Service Publishing Services for Christian Authors, Artists &
Ministries: Books, eBooks, Audiobooks, Music, Screenplays, Film & Curricula

THE TRILOGY OF WISHBONE HOLLOW

VOLUME I

LAST BORN:
A NOVEL OF HISTORICAL FICTION

ISBN: 978-1-61314-747-4

Cover Design & Interior Layout: Innovo Publishing, LLC

Printed in the United States of America
U.S. Printing History
First Edition: 2021

CONTENTS

BACKGROUND

Writ by a neighbor livin' just southeast of the Moffats.

We live in Wishbone. We're thinkin', most of us, that is, that they named the town that for the way the two valleys converged, leavin' that knobby hill right up there lookin' down on God and everybody.

"The rest on us thought it was because of all the ridges and hollows in northern Arkansas that they might'a flat run out'a names for any new towns... My thinkin' is, I could go either way on that, for a fact.

"Of them two valleys, Possum Creek was the biggest on account of it gets its water from Big Mouth Cave. It's a gusher, I can tell you. Best not to try to stand up in the water right there at the mouth.

"The other valley has Tarantula River, and we don't know why it's a river and not even as big as Possum Creek, but right there at the bottom them two rivers team up to make Little Mulberry. That river don't get to be Big Mulberry until it gets joined up with North Fork comin' around the other mountain.

"So right down there at the point'a that Wishbone-shaped valley there was a spot of ground almost big enough to make a town if the buildings weren't too big. Some of the businesses sort'a ran the back'a their buildings up against the hill, and it made 'em cheaper, cooler and warmer in the summer and winter. Leastwise that's what they bragged.

"Way back years ago, we heard that folks got a few teams of mules and a couple'a dirt slips and pushed off that point both ways and then rocked up the sides of them rivers. They had extra rocks to get rid of anyway. Any leftover dirt got sent down Possum Creek. We figured that extra dirt'd end up in Oklahoma where they could make good use of it... maybe make 'em a hill or two.

"And that's the short of how we got this book writ and called *Wishbone Hollow*. Where we referred to the KJV Good Book, we put an asterisk (*) just so you'd know."

(Every part of this book is fiction, and there is no resemblance intended toward any person, living or dead.)

LAST BORN

Rowenna's future destination was pretty much set when she received the Christmas book as a gift for her tenth Christmas birthday. Bernard and Loretta Moffat made it a point to give a Christmas book to each child every year as long as each of the youngens was at home. After that, he (or she) was on his own.

An even dozen youngens seemed to be a handy number for a family, so it was thought that Rowenna's sister, Jadeen, was intended to be the last of the family, but when you get a good thing a'goin' it could be a chore to get it stopped. Besides that, as precarious as it was living on the steep mountains, one should plan on an extra kid to 'make up for the one lost over the hill'.

Growing kids in Arkansas was rather like growin' morning glory flowers. They look good on the fence, but when they're climbin' the cornstalks, chokin' off the tomatoes, and trippin' the horse a'tryin' to plow 'em out, then it might be good to take another look at 'em.

So Jadeen had her nose out of joint for a while, they say. But then she saw the value of someone littler to blame with breakage and other disobediences. Another thing… it was number thirteen girl who thought up the idea of callin' her 'Jade', and that boosted her rating up a notch.

And then their pa, who may not have been the busiest bee in the hive, must have listened to Ma and her bit of wise reasonin'. "Just look at it this way, Bernard; if you were thinkin' on someone bein' around for our old age, forget that. Just look around and see how the youngens are gettin' away faster'n we can produce 'em.Sophia's headed off to Fayetteville, and Laverne is packin' up to go somewhere. Only thing that's kept her here this long is the stage plays."

And Pa seemed to have said, "Loretta, my little sweet pea, it could be you got somethin' there."

Kid number eleven, Laverne, was arguably one of the best heroines the Wishbone Hollow Magic Curtain Theater ever had. She could die and leave the audience weeping and sopping up their tears. Also lining up at the door to see her do it again.

Laverne outgrew Wishbone and ended up about three hollows and two ridges to the east at a place called Eureka Springs. They made her an offer she couldn't refuse. Sometimes she got to die at two or three theaters at a time if they could just get their schedules of performance right.

But then, right after Jadeen, number twelve, was born, here came Rowenna, pink as a baby piglet and dimpled as a brand new golf ball. It soon became evident that she possessed the Moffat hard-headedness.

The people of Wishbone shook their collective heads. No good would come of that, for everyone knew that thirteen was an unlucky number… especially for a Moffat, who was related to the Hopkins. All except Granddad Hopkins, actually the retired Reverend Irvin Hopkins, Rowenna's maternal grandfather.

Preacher Hopkins was actually retired from the local church, but his words around town still carried a lot of weight. Two other relatives sided with him in defense of number thirteen, and they were his two widowed sisters, Sophrenia and Cecilia, who ran the Thimbles and Spools sewing shop along with their cousin, Georgiana.

As the parents were still rather busy with kids number seven to twelve, the older generation had a chance to cast their influence over that last child… number thirteen. The old ladies had room for her to crawl about in their workplace, and Granddad was handy for an afternoon to sit with Rowenna and her cousin Wally, a year and a half older.

Back to the Christmas gift book and its permanent influence on Rowenna. The little girl got her first Christmas book at age two and ate pages seven through ten before she recognized the dog, cat and piggy pictures on the pages. By that time, Laverne, the actress, had learned to read a few words and pointed to them as she read the one-sentence stories to her sister.

Rowenna was hooked. Robert, who was next older than Laverne, could read quite well, loved a challenge and took on the word recognition effort. By age four, Rowenna was receiving 'real' books and reading them without much assistance.

Also at about age four, she discovered the value of her cousin, Wally, five and a half, and they stuck together like a pair of magnets. Maybe it was their size at first, but later, it was identical interests. Wally was a belated chick hatched after four teenage sisters had practically flown the nest. Their mothers being sisters-in-laws, naturally these two youngest were flung together at family gatherings and at church and such.

THIMBLES AND SPOOLS

One particular location in the town of Wishbone was both home and the place of business of two widowed sisters and their cousin.

The house originally belonged to Georgiana, but it would be unseemingly for one old lady to be alone, so Sophrenia and Cecilia moved in with her. There was plenty of room, of course, as that was where Georgiana had reared her family. Six rooms close to the foot of the hill. It was not intended that they be in the center of town, but Main Street sort of crowded in between her house and Possum Creek. So there they were, right in the thick of it all.

Handy, though. They just added a display room to the parlor and stocked it with every known item required by anyone who sewed... along with trimmings and thread... and they were in business. A few patterns rounded out the offering, except for the hand-pieced quilts mostly bought by the 'summer people'.

Good advertisement, it was, to have the quilting frame hanging from the ceiling to be admired by the 'summer trade' who wandered into the shop. It was even more enticing when the three gray-haired ladies, with the proper number of wrinkles, were wielding a needle at the time. The quilt in the frame, however, was not, and likely would never be, for sale. It was purely for show. The ladies were nothing if not showmen… beg pardon, show ladies.

The shelves were laden with beautifully pieced and quilted coverlets made by skillful hands living all the way up the hills in every direction and a few from the nearby hollows. The ladies of Thimbles and Spools made their money on commission sales, and they were master salespersons.

So, back to Rowenna and Wally. The pair were grand-niece and nephew to the three old ladies and were welcome guests. They created the need to keep the cookie jar full. The two well-known children from well-known families created conversation material for the three as well as other locals. And conversation was the 'mother's milk' of mountain relationships.

A pair of wooden rocking horses had their stable under the accounts desk and made trips around and under the quilting platform manned by the trio. The horses themselves were advertisement for the carpenter shop over on Larkspur Lane.

Any comment from 'summer people' on the attractive wooden creatures (authentic from teeth to mane to tail to painted hoofs) produced a business card for 10% off on the purchase of one. Of course, any customer could get at least 10% off on any purchase, but 'summer people' were not supposed to notice that.

When the team of Rowenna and Wally were six and seven and a half, they were fully trusted to make the short trip to the WM (Wilkinson's Market) for some little item the ladies were out of. Like everyone else in Wishbone, the ladies 'ran a tab' at the market. It simplified matters, because small children could then perform the shopping trips without the use of, and possible loss of, actual coins.

The fact that the small town was transverse twice by small mountain rivers brought home the fact that coins dropped in the water could be more or less considered to arrive somewhere over in Oklahoma. This fact also necessitated that each child learn to swim almost as soon as he could walk.

When the team was eight and nine and a half, they were trusted to make a trip over to the Big Three for a ready-made lunch for the

Thimbles ladies. Age and excessive poundage, gradually acquired over the years, made unnecessary trips rare as long as a pair of young legs were available. And all it cost was a pair of ice cream cones while they were there.

The Big Three consisted of three small diners, each offering specialty items only and located in almost the dead center of town

To start the food conversation, Sophrenia quietly mentioned, "What's for lunch?" which was short for "It's too hot to cook, and the youngens want ice cream."

Georgiana, after a polite pause, countered with, "Well… if we've got nothing started, I could go for a piece of fried chicken."

That was not a surprise to the other two, and she usually ordered the wishbone even though it was priced higher. Cecelia, who rather liked a surprise sometimes, alternated her orders.

"I believe I'll have the soup. When I send the pint jar, I get more than when I get it in that there paper bowl."

"It's not paper, I keep saying. It's a formed cellulose container."

Cecelia nodded. "Yeah, like I said… that paper bowl. It's the same stuff that the paper wasps use for their hives, only it isn't made with wasp spit."

"Right, but we don't know what the bowl maker uses. Maybe it's his own…."

"Hush," shouted Sophrenia with her fingers in her ears. "I don't want to hear that. It's nasty, and we're about to eat."

"Not if you don't decide what you want."

Sophrenia, with an injured sniff, "I already know. I want cold ham and slaw. It's too hot for hot food."

Cecelia, with a toss of her gray ringlet hair, "I hadn't noticed anything ever bein' very hot by the time those two get back here, crossin' Possum Creek and all."

Then Georgiana, with a whisper, suggested, "Better than goin' there ourselves, remember? And none of us seemed to want to fire up the stove."

Rowenna and Wally continued to sit on the porch, swinging their bare feet over the edge and waiting for the words to settle and preparing their tastes for ice cream. This banter of words was a game perfected over the years. The game was well-known by the children and all three ladies knew the rules and there was never a winner.

Georgiana decided she'd also have slaw, and Cecelia would have a biscuit, please, and she'd flavor it with her own jelly.

The matter now settled, Rowenna ducked inside the store for the soup jar and the cloth bags for the food, and they were off, bare feet padding the worn paths and the very warm boards of the bridge over Possum Creek. They skipped along in the shade of the store awnings to the path over to the Big Three huts.

The home-churned ice cream turned out to be chocolate today... a favorite. There was never a choice of flavors. You ate what was made for that day, or you didn't. Almost everyone ate. The ice cream hut was very skilled in its specialty and used actual cream, sweetening it with half bee-tree honey and half sugar, and their chocolate was the brown powder that came from a fifty-gallon keg, ordered in by the WM especially for this customer.

The children did not loiter over the ice cream. It was to be eaten quickly or it became liquid... though it was still very tasty when the last drops were drunk from the bowl. Collecting the ordered items from various of the three huts, they were off again.

The pair, racing along on a 'high' from the sugar and fat, felt they had been well paid for their services.

Cecelia peered with interest at her soup. Always thick with vegetables and flavored with meat broth, it was also always a surprise.

Like the flavor of the ice cream, the variety of the soup was entirely the choice of the maker... and if you didn't want that flavor, there was always home-prepared chili with beans that was always made exactly the same way. It was made from a 'secret recipe,' and no chili-lover had ever complained. Or at listened to if they did.

The lady with her gray-streaked hair in a knot on her head smiled with satisfaction. Broccoli, squash, and corn in a tomato broth flavored with the leftover sausages ground into a pulp. A favorite.

Summer people usually viewed it with a puzzled frown the first time they ate it, but only the first time. Any decent soup connoisseur would give it a 5-star rating without a second thought.

Food delivered, the messengers scurried off for further summer amusement, and their great aunts bowed their heads over their food.

It was their habit to be thankful…. mostly for the bountiful blessings from their Lord, but partly because they didn't have to heat up the kitchen. Firing up the wood-burning stove wasn't so bad in the winter… in fact, it was quite cozy, but come summer… well, that was another story!

GRANDDAD HOPKINS

Though he had been retired for more than five years, the old man still felt a kinship with the church that he had helped to erect. Somehow it seemed to be as much a part of his family as the dirt between the two streams of water that came together to make the wishbone shape of the town. Necessary real estate surgery required that much of the mound of dirt must to be scraped away to make a level foundation.

Several donated mule-drawn dirt-slips spent days… yea, weeks… on the project. Help from ANY source was begged for the many and varied jobs, the greatest of them being the laying aside of all useable stones that were uncovered.

The mountains of northern Arkansas could yield a massive amount of what was once volcanic rock. The hard mineral chunks came in all-broken-up shapes and also in massive boulders the sizes of the mules themselves. Centuries of being impregnated with minerals had painted the stones with various colors and patterns.

A fact was, one had to do something with the stones, and the building must be constructed of something, so an argument could be made that God had provided the durable chunks of this material specifically for his house.

Usable stones laid aside, the unusable remains were piled for use in walling off the streams and filling in holes. Like so many of the first buildings in that mountainous area, soil was scraped down from the uphill side to fill in on the lower side to make what was hoped to be a fairly level building plot.

So the Wishbone Congregational Community Church was born on a scrap of useless, donated land and carefully reared into a solid building that would seat at least 75 standard-sized people and provide standing room for almost that many more when necessary.

Local labor created the benches and pulpit and closed off a couple of rooms for children's classes. A stockroom was hooked onto the rear for whatever seemed not to fit anywhere else, and that room acquired the name "Office" and was loosely used for that purpose by the current pastor.

With great thanks to his Creator, the recently licensed Irvin Hopkins had moved in, so to speak. Actually, he lived with his wife and family across Tarantula River, sometimes called Spider River. Tarantula sounds too dangerous. A small, wooden footbridge joined his front yard to that of his beloved church.

All of that was then… and now it was later.

So now Granddad, the preacher, was retired, and when the pair, Rowenna and Wally, reached ten and eleven and a half, it was time for Granddad to take over some of the responsibility for their training that was being ignored by the tolerant great aunts.

The first duty they were taught to assume was care of the church yard. Somehow among the stones there came an everlasting crop of something called a sand burr.

Now, Granddad Irvin was ever the preacher, and he saw spiritual lessons in just about everything, but the clearest and easiest to understand was the sand burr.

"Come over here, youngens, and we're gonna look at this plant. God had a reason for it or it wouldn't be here, so I reckon it is here for a lesson."

Wally immediately found something to object to. "Ah, Granddad, we done saw those things, a'pickin' 'em outta our feet."

"I know that, but now you're gonna see 'em a different way. See here how those blades look just like the grass all around 'em? Well, that's the way sin is. It sneaks in without callin' attention to itself, and it don't make burrs right off. It's gonna wait till it has good roots and can make a lotta burrs so fast that no one can pick 'em all off."

The girl and boy hunkered down beside Granddad, looking at the innocent-looking plant in a different light. Rather clever of it… it seemed.

Granddad continued. "And see here how those blades get thick and spread out, bein' shorter than the other grass, so it don't get itself mowed down? It's hidin', just like sin. And see here where the joints are on the stem? It's tryin' to put down new roots, so it can use up more of the nutrition in the ground. Just like sin takes up a lot of a fellow's time… if he lets it."

The two pairs of young eyes now viewed the clever plant with even greater respect.

"And another thing. See here how I can gather all those blades together and pull, and they break off in my hand, leavin' the root right there in the ground. Can you guess what that reminds me of?"

They turned their eyes to Granddad, shaking their head. There was no way they, with their limited experience, could guess what Granddad could be thinking of.

The old man nodded with satisfaction. There were very few occasions so satisfying as having two pairs of your young flesh-and-blood family hanging onto your every word.

"That reminds me of how some folks think they can just be good all by theirselves and that God will not notice they still have their old sinful nature that they were born with. That plant is tryin' to fool us into thinkin' it's been killed, but I'm going to put a marker right here, and we'll look at it next week."

They were now even more impressed. Imagine…! That was a really smart weed.

Granddad nodded with emphasis. "That there's like some folks thinkin' God won't notice their old sin nature. But they're wrong there. God knows, and until folks' sins are forgiven, they can't even ask God for help to get rid of them. Now come on over here and see this."

Granddad moved over a couple of yards and knelt down by another sand burr plant. Taking his sharpened Winchester knife from his pocket, he straightened the longest blade. The sharp shininess of it sparkled in the morning sun.

The old man's fingers gathered the blades of the plant and thrust his knife into the ground beside the roots. Slicing sideways, he severed the roots below the ground and lifted the plant and clod together. Two pairs of eyes examined the hole and watched Granddad knock back the dirt into the hollow space.

"Lookie here, now. See that bunch'a roots? Almost like a brush for being so many. That plant really wanted to grow there, but my knife wouldn't let it. That there's the way God is with his words. They're like that knife and he is like my hand. He's done told us what to do and how to do it, so now we have the book he had some men write down. That book is the knife to cut away the roots of sin after we ask God for forgiveness."

He looked squarely into each of the pairs of eyes. Yes, it looked like this lesson took… but he'd have another chance at them next week when they examined the marked plant. Bright youngens… these two. He was planning to be proud of them as they grew up. That might take some effort on his part, but he was ready for whatever it took.

"Now, we could go over to the Big Three and have ice cream. It's time they got it made, but there is a problem.…"

"Problem…?" Surely he would not disappoint them after that long, absorbing lesson.

The old man sighed with resignation. "Bein' that both'a you don't like fresh peach ice cream, there'll be no use goin' over there."

"Aw, Granddad…!" and they pounded their fists lovingly on the old man's shoulders and each reached for a hand to help him to his feet. Getting him up was a bit dicey… sometimes… but once he got going, he was fine.

Granddad paid for the ice cream and walked on to the 'spit and whittle bench' where a few others his age were gathered. The older fellows often gathered there to watch the 'summer people' go by… and to wonder, with many words, what the world was coming to.

Ice cream was hardly in their stomachs until the pair of eyes met and the suntanned faces grinned. Idea! They'd pull one over on Granddad and go peek at that plant with the stake by it and see what it was doing.

As it turned out, it was doing nothing, so it was instantly dropped from their mind in favor of something more exciting… like heading down to Little Mulberry River. Not so little, actually, and certainly the water depth was over their heads.

As much water as there was in Wishbone, it was important that all the little ones could swim, and Rowenna and Wally were no exception. There were no restrictions on their wanderings, and water had magnetism for most of the town's children.

The only persons on the bank of Little Mulberry were an older man (a grandpa, no doubt) and two small children on the pier. They were apparently going to be taken for a boat ride… as grandpa was taking what looked like a food basket and other items from a wagon to be transferred to the boat, now tied alongside.

The two small children stood impatiently on the pier, and as Grandpa was so slow, the little boy pulled the boat over to the pier and helped the younger little girl into it. Then he untied the knot of the restraining line.

Rowenna and Wally looked at each other with wide eyes. THAT WAS JUST NOT DONE! Anyone should have known that was not done, even the little boy who might have been as old as six. The girl, however, was more like three and could be forgiven.

Little Mulberry had a rather swift current in the center… being force-fed by two mountain streams, one of them springing from Big Mouth Cave.

As the flat-bottomed craft nosed into the current, it whirled around to follow the flow, and the little girl, now trying to stand and hold to the side of the boat, was pitched forward, screaming, as she looked down at the water….

The little fellow on the bank realized what he should not have done and yelled, "Grandpa! Grandpa! Come help!"

Grandpa, however, was busy and called back, "Just be patient. I'll be there."

By that time, Rowenna and Wally were on the pier and frantically looking from the busy man to the girl in the boat. The current took another turn with the boat, flinging the little girl into the water, immediately sucking her down.

Wally grabbed off his straw hat and thrust it at Rowenna. Palms together, he executed a swan dive that turned into a kingfisher's splash, slicing through the surface. Straight to the bottom he pulled, and he could be seen through the clear water as he plowed toward the girl.

She bobbed to the surface but not head-first. All that was seen of her was the seat of her panties plastered to her round bottom. That tumble pushed her out of the stronger part of the current, and the empty boat went bobbing on down the river, whirling and jogging along at will.

Rowenna had run to the old man and gotten his attention. Together they dashed to the pier and the screaming boy, tears flowing down both cheeks.

The man seemed frozen in time, trying to comprehend it all, and the flowered dress appeared again, this time being lifted up out of the water. As it was raised up, a head and a pair of shoulders appeared beneath.

A couple of strong eleven-and-a-half-year-old arms reached out for the armfuls of water that pulled him toward the shore and quieter water. The girl frantically grabbed at Wally and plastered herself along his shoulders.

The bank of the river was so brushy with sprouts and vines that it was impossible for the old man to reach them to help, so he waited breathlessly as the pair moved toward the pier.

Reaching down, he lifted the little girl from the boy's shoulders, just as she began coughing and sputtering from the water and screaming indignation at the top of her healthy lungs.

The old man had tears streaming down his wrinkled cheeks and stared speechlessly at the two children. Wally stood dripping a puddle of Little Mulberry creek onto the worn boards of the pier as his cousin put his hat back on his head.

When the man found words, he thanked them profusely and insisted on a reward.

Wally shrugged it away. "You wasn't gonna get here in time, so I did. It weren't nothin'...."

"Yes, it was something. Tell me what you would like to have, and I'll get it for you."

"What... well, I don't know." And that was the honest truth. When one had everything, as Wally had, then what was there to want? He looked at his cousin for help, and she was thinking. Forehead in frowns and eyes clenched. Mouth screwed up trying to think of something this man, who so fiercely wanted to give something, could give.

Then, with a flip of the head… maybe she had it. Leaning forward, she whispered into Wally's still-wet ear. The boy brightened and nodded. Why not…?

"Mister, if it was you wantin' so bad to give me something, I could tell you this. My granddad was who taught me to swim under water so I could go faster. If you was wantin' to give somethin', we know what he really wants. It's something he wanted even before I was born."

Rowenna, her face wreathed in smiles, was nodding happily. "It's true, Mister. It's something Granddad has always wanted and couldn't get."

"And what would that be…?"

"Windows."

"Windows…?"

Wally came to the rescue. "Its them colored windows, you know, with glass colored into pictures…? It'd be for the church that got built a long time ago, and it has plain glass windows. Granddad has always wanted those windows that shone colored light through 'em when the sun shone."

The man finally nodded. "You're describing stained glass windows, I believe. Does your granddad live close by?"

Rowenna again. "Yes, sir. He'd be up the street at the spit and whittle bench."

"The… what…?"

Then Wally. "You know! The place where men sit to talk about what happened a long time ago. We could show you."

And that's when the five persons climbed up the small hill to the city and the bench. To put it mildly, they attracted attention. The drenched child whose wet clothing was soaking that of her grandpa, and there was the boy with sodden overalls.

It took some arguing, because Preacher Hopkins did not hold with being paid for such a kindness, but the man would not be satisfied until he had been shown the church and had measured the windows.

In due time, the wagon came down the hill from the graveled road up on the ridge and asked for directions. The thing was, he was already standing in the church yard, though it was hard to tell it from other buildings.

After the brilliantly colored windows were installed, that suddenly changed. No one with two eyes could mistake it for anything but a church, and maybe only one eye would be needed.

As the installer turned his team toward the road that led out of the hollow, the retired Reverend Irvin Hopkins stood at the point of the wishbone and looked toward the south as though his eyes would never get enough of the sight of those windows.

It was only his two grandchildren who were close enough to hear him sigh wistfully. "Now, all we need is a bell and bell tower."

Rowenna looked at Wally, and he shrugged and looked back. Sometimes there just wasn't no way to please some people.

The current minister, young Preacher Harvey Clemmons, who was sent to Wishbone Hollow to get experience so he could be sent to a bigger place, took special notice of these two. If that gift was the way they felt about the church, then they should be given special jobs.

There was that in-ground marquee that spelled out reminders to the town as a whole, and the message must be changed every week. That would be a good job for that young man.

Now what about the ten-year-old girl...? Well, he had been thinking he needed someone in charge of the books.

Not, of course, to count the money and post the records. She was much too young for that. What he needed was someone to inspect and repair the damage done to the songbooks each week. Being well-used when they were given to the church, they had begun to deteriorate further.

There was the job of removing tatters, and if the lost hymn was a favorite, it must be found in one of the extra books that had completely fallen apart and pasted over a song that was not popular. Then a notation must be made on the adjoining sheet from where it disappeared, directing the singer to the page number of the new location.

That was just about the size of a job for her. For several years, it remained her job. She was a lot older before the church was able to buy brand new... never used before... song books.

THREE YEARS LATER

It is necessary to back up for a moment. As Wally's pa had gotten himself killed from infection due to an accident with a bobcat trap, Granddad Hopkins took special pains to spend time with him, and that involved teaching him how to use a gun.

As the cousins were so often together, Granddad expanded his training to include Rowenna when she could barely fit a 22mm Winchester in her small, strong hand.

These two… the boy from a house full of females… and little number thirteen at the end of a hard-working family with tired parents… became the old granddad's special charges, and regular target practice at that young age created amazing accuracy. It was on the girl's eleventh birthday that he presented them both with their own guns.

Granddad deduced that Wally, being a boy, would need one sooner or later, and little number thirteen was prone to wander the woodlands, and eventually she would come upon a bobcat or a mountain rattler.

Then, at Rowenna's twelfth Christmas, her mom was somewhat at loss for an interesting book for her… what with the many books that already lined the Moffat walls from gifts to her siblings. Watching advertisements, she located the book on Florence Nightingale and her struggles to become a nurse in a man's war. It was said to be an interest to young teenage girls, and Ma thought that described Rowenna.

Now back to three years later.

The girl, being so far down the line in birth, had no regular, every day duty now that she had finished the eight years of school. When there were no weeds to pull or vegetables to pick for the canners, she had a fair amount of free time.

Her home on the top of a hill had many trees but the best trees were in the valley at Granddad's old place across Spider River from the church. Oaks and sassafras grew thick behind his house, and as the hill climbed upward there were dogwoods and wild plums, hickory and walnut… and an impressive number of chinky pin trees. Outsiders spelled the trees by the difficult French pronunciation of chinquapin, but the natives of Arkansas pronounced it the way they thought it should be.

Possibly that latter interesting tree grew in many of the southern states, but Arkansas must have produced some of the best. With trunks often three feet in diameter and peaks reaching sixty feet in the air, they clung tenaciously to the boulders often twice the size of a two-hole privy.

The nuts produced by the chinky pin tree were possibly a wild version of the Chinese chestnut, though how that could have happened is anyone's guess. The tree put forth clumps of flowers that turned into clusters of burrs the size of a hen egg… each tightly enclosing a marble-sized kernel in a thin, woody sheath.

The nuts were a favorite for fattening hogs, who seemed to relish the whole stickery burr as well as the oil-rich kernel. Late in the fall, the burrs split open and the 'chestnuts' began to fall. A strong breeze would bring down a sprinkling of them, and an overnight gale could spread layers of nuts covering all the ground around.

Children were sent with pails to gather them, as they were a valued snack the rest of the year and were very handy for creating richness in Christmas fruitcakes.

Rowenna had been given the assignment that… sometime when she was downtown at Granddad's… she must go on up the hill and gather a winter supply. And she fully intended to do that, but to bring back enough nuts, she must saddle one of Granddad's horses and take the saddlebags.

To get the good ones, one should gather early, before the hundreds of squirrels got to them, and the deer, who also liked them, tromped them into the ground. This little chore nagged at the girl, but the current problem was… she had a brand new book about a nurse called Clara Barton.

She was not, however, planning to read THAT book, as she had her own way of prolonging pleasure. One of the world's most perfect feelings, she knew, was to have something to read that she knew she loved… and to also have another 'something' that she was sure she would also like. That was almost an embarrassment of wealth.

So today she had brought her book on Florence Nightingale about her experiences in the Crimean war. She had only read it twice, and the knowledge that she had another book waiting in the pipeline to read would greatly increase her pleasure in this third reading about the brave nurse.

She would take one of the collie dogs for company and climb up into her favorite oak tree to read. This tree had a wonderful swing with a long rope, but for reading, she preferred sitting on the limb.

The tree was so terribly large that it would have been impossible to climb without a ladder… except for the elm sapling nearby. One must climb up the elm all the way to its limber tip, then lean the tip over far enough to step on an upper limb of the oak. Then she could work her way down to the 'swing' limb for her favorite reading place.

This was the how she and Wally had hung the swing more than five years ago. Since then, she had pounded a few handy nails on the elm that made the climb even easier.

One of the collie pups was eager to go with her, because he liked to nap on the swing board. His name was Stub, but that wasn't his name until he caught the tip of his tail in a wolf trap. Stub was a happy dog and frantically wagged his half-tail to signal his willingness to accompany her.

"Come on, Stub," was all the encouragement he needed. So the girl, with her 22mm Baby Winchester in her dress pocket as she was instructed to do by Granddad, picked up her book and headed for the swing tree almost a half a mile away.

It was an early fall day, and the weather was so delicious it seemed one could eat it with a spoon… if they had a mouth that was big enough.

As she walked along with the excited dog running circles here and there, her mind played over a session she had recently had with her three great aunts at the Thimbles and Spools.

It was evident that they had given a great deal of thought to how to bring up this subject… one that the girl's mother should have taken care of… but obviously had not. No matter. The aunts were accustomed to being forced to do this sort of pick-up duty when it was ignored by negligent parents. They were skillful and should have been… as there was a lot of negligence that must be made up.

The three aunts had 'invited' her to sit at the round table. That was the first indication that a lecture was coming. The cookie jar with her favorite nut-and-chocolate cookies was on the table, and that was the second indication.

The next and most noticeable indication was that the aunts had trouble getting their words started. A few knowing glances at each other and finally Aunt Sophrenia began.

"Rowenna, sweetheart…."

Now, that was the dead giveaway. She was often called 'Rowenna, baby…' but never 'Rowenna, sweetheart…'. She resisted the impish desire to grin, but out of love and respect, she firmed her lips, looked downcast and reached for a cookie. She owed a lot to these ladies, and she loved them intensely. To continue….

"…Sweetheart, we've been thinking. We're sure your mother would have thought of this, but she is so very busy with everything she has to do, it would be best for us to mention it to you… now that you are thirteen years old."

The other two aunts nodded, and Cecelia added, "That's true, darling, and a lovely thirteen you are. I see your ma has let down your dress hems, and that is very becoming. Now there are other things…."

Rowenna was sure there was.

"We have noticed how rapidly you walk when there is no need. That makes your skirt front swing between your knees quiet unattractively. I'm sure you have more pettislips, and if you haven't, then we can make some for you. An extra pettislip of heavier fabric would hold your skirt smoothly in front…."

Aunt Georgiana now felt free to butt in. "And, sweetheart, if you wouldn't walk so fast, that would hardly happen. Now that you're thirteen."

More head nodding and a lot of pleasant smiling to show that there were no hard feelings on their part. They were just doing their duty, however uncomfortable it made them.

"And about your pocket. Perhaps your next skirts should have no pocket because you tend to fill them so full, they bulge and swing along like you are carrying a satchel."

Rowenna tightened her lips. If only they knew! The 22mm was small but a bit chunky, and if the aunts knew what was weighing down her pocket, she might have to apply the smelling salts to bring them back to breathing.

They must never know. Granddad had sworn her to secrecy. Her parents, of course, knew and approved. It was something they would have done sooner or later, and it was good that Granddad did it for them.

"But there was one good thing we noticed, sweetheart." This, of course, was a good strategy. If she must be scolded, they would end up with a compliment.

Aunt Georgiana fielded this one. "We have noticed that you have given up climbing trees. That was very wise. It would be quite unseemingly to see a girl of thirteen climbing up a tree as you and Wally did when you were small."

The word 'small' was emphasized. There were smiles all around the table, and Aunt Cecelia poured her a cup of tea. Her favorite… flavored strongly with dried orange peel. It was delicious! It went perfectly with the chocolate cookies. Rowenna lowered her eyes and plastered on one of her sweetest smiles.

"I thank you for reminding me. I'll try to remember."

And now, she was walking up the beginning of the hill with her gun in her pocket and her book in her hand with every thought and intention on climbing into the 'reading tree' and enjoying her afternoon.

She fully kept her promise… she was remembering. Those were three of the sweetest old ladies she knew, and she was lucky to have so many who cared for her. But not climb trees… ? Perish the thought!

THE CHINKY PIN CAVE

It was still easy to climb up to her reading perch, but would have been easier… and safer… if her skirt had not been lengthened, and she had not had to wear the one pettislip her mother insisted on.

Gun in pocket and book in hand. She settled herself on the wide limb where she could lean back against the trunk. The bark of the tree trunk had been smoothed from years of wear and was very comfortable at her back. Hitching up her knee to help hold the book, she lowered a toe to the swing rope just to remind Stub that she was up there.

Collies were not particularly known for being bodyguards, but they were companions by nature and had very sharp hearing. If there was a foreign noise, the girl wanted to know about it and Stub would tell her.

Stub loved to climb into the swing and doze on the board. Most likely, it was the challenge he liked, because it took a number of tries before he could land himself just right… or it could have been that the elevated position gave him a better viewpoint. Also, it might have kept the lizards from racing over his back.

So while he dozed with one eye open, the girl read with a mind that wandered. Through her head kept drumming 'chinkpin cave, chinkpin cave.' She tried to push it away and stubbornly re-read the paragraph.

A bird in a neighboring tree whistled "CHinky piN! CHinky piN!" A screeching cricket overhead said "Cheeeeey Piiiiin."

A crow flew overhead screaming, "Cave! Cave! Cave!"

That was the trouble with a chore that you put off. It kept hanging there in your mind like a spider making a web. When you tore down the web, two minutes later there it was again.

She could do that chore today, but she'd have to go back to Granddad's house and get a horse and the saddle bags. If she went all the way up there to the cave, she might just as well get a winter's supply.

Grabbing up a handful of dress and skirt and tucking it under her chin, she backed down the elm, feeling for the familiar limbs and nails with her toes to reach the ground.

"Come on, Stub. We got work to do."

Coming through the horse pasture, she selected Mustard… her favorite. He was about as near yellow as a horse can ever get, and he was just about as nippy. There was something about him that Rowenna liked. Leading him by the mane, they made their way the barn and the saddle and bridle. The huge saddle bags would hold a good half a bushel of nuts on either side.

Jumping aboard, she whistled for the dog, and they were off. Strangest thing! She kept thinking about the sermon last Sunday. It was one she had heard dozens of times, but there it was again. Little boy Samuel was trying to sleep and kept hearing a voice.

Now what did that have to do with hearing a crow and a cricket and another bird she couldn't recognize? She was quite certain she was not being called to lead the country, as Samuel had been. But there it was. So she'd just go get those pesky chinky pins and get it over with. Only way to shut that voice up.

The preacher had followed those words with the admonition that often angels were assigned to carry messages from God to humans; if the humans just stayed attuned to him, these messages would have meaning. When that happened, it would be best for the human to listen.

So what did it mean to be 'attuned'? The preacher didn't go on to explain that. Maybe the grown-ups already knew.

Mustard plodded his way up the mountain. He threaded himself skillfully between the boulders and tested with a hoof for small rolling stones. He'd been up this mountain many times, often with this human on his back. Nothing to it! Just be careful.

Stub zigzagged among the boulders and trees, sniffing and snorting... reading the messages of many animals. Then, near the top, he stopped... pricked up his ears... and pointed his nose to the sky. With a meaningful howl, he set out diagonally across the mountain toward the cave.

Now, why would he do that? He'd been to the cave many times, and it was not exactly an exciting place for a dog. Flat floor. Cool, rock-lined walls. Tiny rivulet of clear water that seeped from a rock ledge. Just a cool place for a kid to rest in the summer.

Clicking a bit more speed from Mustard, she followed the dog. So far, she could only hear the birds and crickets and an occasional nut dropping to the leaf-litter. Squirrels raced along limbs in every direction.

She watched the squirrels, picturing squirrel stew running around on four dainty feet... but not today. This was to be the chinky pin day.

But that was not to be.

As she neared the cave, she caught faint sounds of a small animal in distress, and it came from the direction of the cave...

maybe. Here in the mountains, echoes often played tricks on the ears, but there were too many trees about to even get a good echo.

Sound coming from the cave, for sure. Halting the horse near a tree and tying his rein, she took the 22mm from her pocket and crept silently across the deep leaf-litter. Stub was snorting from excitement but staying with her... which meant the sound was not an animal he recognized.

The girl's good sense told her she should turn quietly, return to the horse and go down the mountain... but there were times she did not listen to her good sense. SOMETHING had made her come to the cave. She'd creep closer and peek around the doorway. Whatever it was, it should have heard her coming and either ran or prepared for attack.

The sound died away and Stub stopped, standing on three paws. Rowenna proceeded slowly. At the wide opening to the cave she stopped, gun in hand, and leaned toward the door. The sound came again, startling her. She knew in an instant what it was, and it was not frightening. It was a very young child who was sniffling and whining, his voice hoarse from screaming.

Calling to Stub, she entered, and when the baby heard her, he started trying to cry again. Closer, Rowenna could see a rope tied around his foot and secured under a fairly large rock. He could crawl for a couple of feet but could not reach the cave door. Or his mother.

He couldn't be here alone, she decided, and she was right. There in the semi-dark interior lay a woman with what looked like blood seeping from her leg and her feet were bare. She did not move or make a sound, and as the girl crept closer, she could see yellow hair matted with something sticky.

Blood! It had to be blood! Now what could she do? She picked up the woman's hand... warm. Fingers at the pulse (something she learned from Nurse Nightingale. First check pulse. Live persons should be tended before the... well, the others).

Her inexperienced finger detected a faint movement. Was that the pulse? If so, that meant she was still alive. And blood was seeping, so that meant her heart was still beating... didn't it...?

So... what could she use to stop the bleeding? Dress sash? She had a sash, but so did the woman. It was tightly sewed, but by stepping on the end and pulling very hard, she loosed one side. Now... blood came from the heart, so the bandage must be between the wound and the heart. But not too tight. How tight was too tight? Oh... why didn't she know more!

The baby had turned toward her... to sit on his soggy, smelly diaper and watch, sniffing and hiccoughing. Rowenna's mind was in a whirl. She could not lift the woman, and that was certain. She had to make a choice, and the baby won the coin toss.

She'd get him on the horse, somehow, and go back to town for help. The rock was easily moved aside, and the rope on his foot was easy to untie. Lifting him, she hugged him tightly against her chest... squirming... and his diaper was dripping and very smelly. No matter.

With Stub on her heels, she struggled back to the horse. Mustard's beautiful brown eyes followed her movement, and he snorted... was she really going to put that thing on him? She was... but that was not the problem.

Her nearly fourteen-year-old arms could not lift him up to the saddle, and he was too small to sit in the saddle without help. Still hugging the disagreeably-smelling little boy, she struggled to the top of the boulder beside Mustard.

Bending over, she tried to sit him on the saddle but could not hold him there while she mounted behind. Studying the problem from various angles, with Stub watching intently, she finally decided to put the little fellow on his tummy and tie him to the saddle horn with the rope that was on his foot.

Mustard did his part and stood patiently. She put the baby tummy down and sat on the edge of the boulder, holding him solidly with her foot while she tied the rope to the saddle horn and wound it under his arms while trying to keep from falling down to the feet of the horse.

Then she made a second loop around the baby at the diaper level and pulled the loose end back to where she hoped she would be sitting... if she could just slide down there onto the saddle bags while holding the rope.

It was a surprise to Mustard when she slipped the last little way and landed with a clunk onto the saddlebags. It would not have been nearly so much trouble if her skirt had not been lengthened and if she was not wearing a bothersome pettislip.

She was on her way down the hill when she realized she could have taken off her pettislip and made a cleaner diaper for the baby... but there was no way to clean him up, so it might not have helped with the smell. Anyway, Mustard was galloping as if his tail was on fire, with Stub running scout.

Down the hill they plummeted with the little fellow screaming in his hoarse voice, but finally he became so exhausted he hung limp arms down one side of the saddle and legs on the other wide and snubbed.

At Granddad's house she walked past his yard, crossed the bridge and into the church yard. No one was noticing... which was good because her dress was up to her thighs on both sides. Right ahead she saw her relief station, Thimbles and Spools.

There might be customers, so she climbed up to the hill to the back door and slid to the ground, Stub still in attendance.

Slipping the rope away from the baby, she eased him off the saddle into her exhausted arms. She'd made it! One thing about the aunts... she could always count on them to know what to do. They did.

They had no bottles, but the little fellow was acquainted with cups and milk. And he was very hungry. Next came washcloths and soap and that was when Rowenna left him.

A quick word with the aunts agreed that as Wally was gone and Granddad was too old, her next best help would be at the WM. There was always someone at the Market, and if Nathan, almost eighteen years old, was there, he would be the best. Quick thinking, he was, and good on a horse.

Mountain people were rapid to understand trouble and jump in to help, because so many things could happen with the water, the terrain and the animals. And the mountain ledges. Within minutes, the strong young man from WM was in the saddle. Spurring the horses forward, they retraced the well-known trail.

The woman was still there and still had a pulse. Maybe. The next problem was how to get her down the hill. Nathan looked her up and down, and decided he could lift her. So fortunate that she was not really big.

So together they hoisted her into his arms and he carried her to the horse. Now what?

Leading his horse to the boulder, he asked Rowenna to see if she could hold the woman up until he got on. Didn't work. So Rowenna slid down behind the saddle and he lifted the woman up. With effort she was held, leaning heavily on Rowenna. Nathan climbed onto the rock and held to her while Rowenna slid down to the ground, at great expense to her modesty.

Settling himself behind the saddle, Nathan lifted the woman with one arm behind her shoulder and the other under her knees. Rowenna put the reins in his hands, and he would attempt to guide the horse to town. It looked as if it might be successful if Nathan's arms held out... and stacking and carrying groceries had given him strong arms. He headed bravely down the hill, his obedient horse doing her part.

Rowenna watched for a couple minutes and then went after her horse to follow after him. That was when she heard conversation back through the trees. Grabbing Mustard's reins, she fairly pulled him along and hid him behind a jutting rock, taller than he was. In case of a showdown, she could never fend off two men. She'd have to sneak around and hope to escape, but even on horseback she could not out-run a bullet.

After hiding the horse, she climbed a sapling and transferred to a limb. Her long skirts were not a bit of help. Hiding behind the tree trunk, she peered toward the cave and saw them approach. Two men. They had apparently tied their horses somewhere back in the trees, because they were on foot, which seemed strange.

She could not see them closely but knew she had never seen them before. She could, however, almost hear their words. Faintly and broken....

No one in the cave... hmmm. Well, for certain the hostages didn't leave by themselves. The rock that was on the baby's rope had been moved. What happened?

Look for a trail. Scuffed leaves. They had to have left a trail, whoever got them. Nodding together, they began to scout around for evidence.

Rowenna could hardly hear them, but she heard enough to know she was in trouble. Eventually they would come to her tree. She had to think quickly within her whirling mind. A 22mm against what had to be two men with guns surely more powerful than hers? Suicide… or maybe murder. Hers.

They came closer but were not together. Leaning away from the trunk far enough to sight through the leaves, she watched as one of the men came closer. He took his gun from his pocket and was holding it loosely, pointing to the ground. The trees were thick here, and it was hard to get a good aim.

But when he bent forward to check the trail, she aimed at a leg. Thigh would be best, and then another shot at his gun hand. If she could. Terribly ambitious plan, but what else was there to do? If they would injure a woman and tie a baby to a rock, what would they do with her…? She was certain she knew.

The man started to straighten up, and she knew it was now or never. With a careful squeeze, it was done. A zing and a yell, and she was again hidden behind the tree trunk. They still had no way of knowing she was above them.

A careful peek showed that she had hit his leg and he was lying on the ground, his gun flung several feet away… out of convenient reach. He instinctively tried to feel for the gun, and she shot into the ground by his hand.

Then on a sudden impulse, she shot into the direction of the other man without taking aim. The man on the ground yelled. "Run for your life. It must be a posse." The man ran.

What now? She had to watch her ammo, and he must not be let to get to his gun. But he still didn't know where she was. If she shot again, he would know she was up the tree, but he might have trouble actually shooting her among all the limbs. He would, eventually, of course.

If only Stub was smart enough to stay with the horse. She could not afford to have him looking up in the tree to find her. She assessed her situation.

Only Nathan knew where she was and he had his hands full... literally.

Nathan had not hurried, knowing Rowenna would catch up to him, but when he looked back and didn't see her, he knew there was trouble. Speeding up as fast as he could, he headed straight for the Thimbles and Spools, managing to slide off the saddle without dropping the woman.

She groaned softly as she was off-loaded onto a bed and out of Nathan's aching arms, and he told the ladies, "I'm goin' back for Rowenna." Without explaining why, he was gone.

Stub was about as confused as Rowenna was scared. Somehow, he instinctively knew to remain where he was put... by the horse.

The girl had three shots left. Would Nathan understand what happened, and why she was not behind him?

The man on the ground examined his bleeding wound that was fast soaking his clothes. He kept looking toward the gun and around in every direction. If he could just get that gun, then he'd start to crawl away and maybe not be seen. Spike would soon be back with help if he could.

With both hands on the ground, the man hoisted his bottom a few inches toward the gun, dragging his wounded leg. He seemed to be able to bear pain quite well. He hoisted himself another few inches. He was going to get there, and it wouldn't take long. That couldn't happen. He must not have that gun.

Taking aim through the limbs, she waited until he was amid-hoist, and fired at his shoulder. No faster than he was moving, she should be able to hit exactly where she aimed, and with a ping, it was done.

He screamed and fell backward, his shirt turning red at the shoulder. She felt a pang of pain, watching him. She hadn't wanted to hurt him... just stop him. She remembered Granddad's warning. "Remember, thou shalt not kill... unless you have to. If it's you or him, be sure to make it him."

She and Wally had stared at their preacher granddad with wide eyes. One thing about Granddad: he was very easy to understand. They had been too small to remember when he was the preacher at the church, but he must have been a good one. He was very plain about what he said.

So she was down to two shots left in the gun and the man was lying on his back, alternately screaming and groaning. She considered escape. She could sidle down the back of the tree and slip around to where she had hidden Mustard.

If she did, help might come and this person might get away, and he was clearly the one who had kidnapped the woman and the baby, and someone… somewhere… was sure to be worried about herself and Nathan. She had two shots left, so she had time. Maybe.

DECISION MADE

She had a little time to think, but every minute seemed an hour. In her whole protected life, she had not faced such a many-faceted problem.

Why had her head told her to gather chinky pins? She still had none, and Mustard's saddle bags were empty. She thought again about little boy Samuel, but that didn't seem to fit. What was that other thing about angels getting assigned to help humans? If she got down from here… no, WHEN she got down from here… she would find that verse and see exactly what it said.

She would get down. She had two shots, and if he reached for the gun, she would shoot his gun hand. She might warn him, and she might not… that would depend on circumstances. She was quite sure she could hit his hand, and if she did not hit it with the first shot, there was another bullet. She was sure he would believe her if she warned him, and if he could not get his gun, he could not shoot her. Decisions… difficult decisions and no one to ask what was best to do. If she could just hold him off, Nathan… or someone… would come…?

That thought comforted her. SOMEONE would come. The aunts would be worried and send someone back. Maybe Wally if he got back to the store. More likely Nathan again. Someone would come.

Nathan's aching arms rippled the reins against his mare's heaving ribs. He wasn't sure what he would find at the cave, but it shouldn't be with a totally exhausted horse. Racing the mare back to the WM, he'd transferred the saddle to a frisky stallion and left with a gallop, yelling to his pa, "Send help to the chinky pin cave!" He was out of sight before his pa could respond.

Down the street to the point of the wishbone, he galloped across the bridge and through Preacher Hopkins' yard and pasture. Joining the trail toward the mountain, he kept the animal at a run. He would have to slow him down when he came to the trees and rocks, but he'd make time now while he could.

He was within a quarter of a mile when he heard the shot. Good news. With a sigh of relief, he hurried on… 22mm… that would be Rowenna. A fellow would have a weapon with more power.

Nathan's pa could see no one he could spare, so he leaped onto the remaining stallion and galloped bare-backed toward the mountain. When he cleared the bridge he caught sight of his son a good three quarters of a mile ahead.

Almost at the top of the hill, Nathan's heart squeezed him breathless with fear. That 22mm could have been the kidnapper; he could have overpowered her and shot her with her gun. He could have wounded her into submission and was carrying her off. If he would kidnap once, he would kidnap again. There was, without doubt, two of them. And one underpowered girl!

When he could see the mouth of the cave, he could not yet see her. "Reena…? REENA! Where are you?"

The girl in the tree saw him, but her courage had drained out into her shoes and she had no voice. Nathan was running through the leaf-litter and he almost stumbled over the prone man, groaning softly and bleeding.

Finally she got a word out… "Nathan…?"

Startled, he looked up. "Reena? What're you doing up there?"

"H-h-h-h-hiding." She stuttered and started to cry. Tears flowed unbidden down her flushed cheeks, and she hated them. She did not want to cry. She had no time or strength to cry.

"Can you come down? I can come up and…."

"No. I can come down." But her feet trembled almost uncontrollably.

Stop it! she told her feet. Reaching the sapling, she started down, her shoe sole fumbling for the limbs while holding an armful of skirt and pettislip up out of the way.

Nathan reached up and guided her feet onto the nail steps, and she dropped her skirts down to a respectable length. Then, ignoring her efforts, he reached up and caught her, one hand on each side of her waist, and lifted her to the ground, standing her on her wobbly feet.

"Your gun, Reena? Where is it?"

"P-p-p-pocket..." And her shaking hand checked to make sure the chunky bulk of it was still pulling her skirt out of shape.

Mr. Wilkinson was kneeling beside the man. "Passed out from pain, I reckon. I'll put him on...."

"Pa, would you put him on your horse and ride mine? I'm takin' Rowenna back to town. She can't hardly stand up, much less ride by herself." Nathan's strong, almost-eighteen-year-old arms lifted the small almost-fourteen-year-old girl into the saddle on Mustard and pulled himself up onto the saddle bags behind her.

"Don't try to think or talk," he instructed. "Just pretend you're a sack of chinky pins on the saddle, and I'm going to hold the sack steady. Hear me?"

She sniffed and nodded. What had happened? She was doing so good... so brave... and remembering all that Granddad taught her, and then she came apart like a lump of sugar in a cup of hot tea. She didn't try to talk on the way back to town, but she decided that would never happen again. Totally embarrassing, it was.

Florence Nightingale had walked into the battlefield and tended wounds with the war going on around her. She took care of hospital rooms and she did everything she had to do. She insisted that everyone wash constantly. Next time something happened, Rowenna would stay brave and be smarter. Just like Nurse Nightingale.

The aunts had closed the showroom and were bustling about. The woman seemed to be coming around, and the baby was crawling on the floor. Rowenna walked in and was descended upon like a junebug spotted by three hungry ducks.

"Oh, my poor dear... are you hurt?"

"Your poor dress is a shambles. Were you...?"

"Are you bleeding...? You didn't get shot, did you...?"

"I'll make you some chamomile tea, my dear. You just sit...."

"You have a sleeve trying to rip out." Aunt Georgiana faced her accusingly, her blue eyes piercing beneath her thick gray brows. Having a ripped sleeve was very near to a sin.

"And the lace on her pettislip is ripped loose... where have you been, child?"

Aunt Sophrenia hugged her and leaned close, whispering in her ear. "Honey, that man... he didn't...?"

When Rowenna could get in a word, this last concern seemed the first one to address. "No, Aunt Sophrenia," she began in a rather loud voice so all could hear. "I was not hurt. I hurt him. I shot him twice, and if he had come at me, I would have shot him again in the face." It felt good to shed some of her outrage.

Dead silence. The room was pin-drop quiet when Nathan stepped into the room. "Reena, I'm gonna go tell your folks you'll be staying here the night. Gonna get Wally to go with me to make sure they believe me."

"Oh, no!" demanded Aunt Cecelia. "Just say she wants to visit. Don't be scarin' her folks... way up on the hill like they are."

Nathan Wilkinson squared his muscular shoulders and faced the gray-haired trio. "Beggin' your pardon, ma'ams. Those are her parents, and they need to know everything that I know. There'd be no way I'd just say she was here for a visit. She was a very brave girl and did everything right no matter how scared she was. Her folks will be proud of her, and I will tell them just how right that will be."

Aunt Cecelia frowned with concern. "But she... used a... gun...?"

Bravely, Nathan stood his ground. "Ma'am, meaning no disrespect, but it just bein' the truth. If she hadn't been taught to use that gun, and if she didn't have it in her pocket, we'd be a'buryin' her in a couple'a days."

"Gun... in her... pocket...?" She turned a knowing look to her relatives, who nodded in unison.

"That's what was wrong with that... pocket...."

Another nod. "And makin' it hang down, crazy-like."

"Good thing she had that gun."

"Wouldn't see how she could know where to shoot."

Nathan thought the conversation needed help that only he could give with the proper emphasis. "Ladies, I can tell you this. She brought blood from his leg and it didn't stop him, so she brought blood from his shoulder. If she says the next bullet would be in the face, that's where it would have been. Chance he'll live, but it's only owin' to her skill. That shoulder wound she made could'a been in his heart. Pa's got 'im in the lockup, but there ain't no one to tend to 'im, so he'll be goin' on to Eureka quick as someone'll take 'im." A pause for beath.

"Now I gotta go. Her folks got the right to know what all happened, and I'm the only one that can tell it. So long, Reena. See you later." And he was gone.

Rowenna stared after him with amazed and puzzled eyes. She had known Nathan Wilkinson all her life, mostly from behind a counter or busily stocking cans on shelves. Now she saw a totally different Nathan. He told everything exactly right, just exactly how it had happened, and she was certain she had never uttered a word on the trip home.

Granddad heard about the hilltop activity and appeared at the Thimbles and Spools. Needed to retrieve his horse, anyway. The old man put an arm around Rowenna's shoulders and tipped his head familiarly against hers. "Good show, youngen. You showed 'em, and you were brave as any soldier in a battle."

Rowenna turned to the wrinkled, proud, smiling face. She whispered, "No, Granddad. I was scared, petrified. I was shakin' so I like'to'a tumbled right out of that tree."

Granddad squenched his faded blue eyes, looked into her very thoughts, and whispered back, "But you didn't. There wasn't never a soldier that had any sense that wasn't petrified and scared, but he still did what he had to do. Now, these ladies will dearly love taking care of you, so let them do it. I dare say your pa'll be down here soon. I'll go now, and you'll know what to do." And he was gone.

As the door closed behind him, Rowenna heard Aunt Sophrenia softly tell her sister, "Cecelia, we must figure a way that girl can carry that gun that won't pull her skirts out of shape."

Rowenna barely had the strength to smile to herself. True to Granddad's prediction, her pa appeared just as she had been tucked into bed with a cup of tea in her hands. The warmth of the cup relaxed her hands, and they had almost stopped tingling.

Pa had red eyes and sniffles. He leaned close and whispered, "My baby girl! What you did was no more than I would have expected of you. That doesn't mean I don't think you're special. I think it was good thing we went ahead and had that thirteenth kid." He stopped to wink and grin conspiratorially. "Leastwise there's a family over to Bentonville that'll think so. They been scrappin' the countryside for that baby and the young woman that was to take care'a him. Thugs stole them two away at gunpoint, the law's thinkin'."

Rowenna brightened. "They've already found…?"

Pa shook his head. "It's been in the paper and posted. The kid's been gone two days. Looks like you might'a took out one'a the kidnappers. He might live… might not. I reckon the young lady'll come around thanks to you. Bentonville folks'll be after her and the kid by tomorrow, I'd wager."

The tea began to take effect, and her eyes were droopy. Pa patted her arm and left to talk with the aunts.

GIRL WITH THE GUN

The Wishbone Cryer emblazoned the headlines across their two-page fold-over newspaper. It was not often they had access to a scoop like this one… with such minute and poignant details that could be furnished by the protagonist's sister.

Jadeen had secured the position of 'copy girl' for the tiny establishment, which was mainly running errands, making the tea or coffee and sweeping out the press room. She also furnished bits of local interest and helped put together the Classified Column.

The very efficient Classified Column was the backbone of the paper. It increased the distribution for two good reasons. One: there might be something there you wanted, so you read it. Two: there were sure to be interesting tidbits tucked within the column, as that was the ONE place everyone looked… so you read it.

But now the Cryer had obtained the scoop of a lifetime. How often did a thirteen-year-old girl wound (read: capture) a kidnapper and rescue two people? An extra press run of the paper was required when the story was demanded by publications in Pleasant Valley, Clifty and Slaughter's Bend. The story was picked up by the Eureka Blaze and even went as far as the Bentonville Sun.

And for Rowenna, being a healthy almost-fourteen-year-old in a country town was a wonderful thing, and the next day she was up and about... all tremors and jitters gone... but a sadness had settled in. Jadeen Moffat, unlike her sister, was enjoying the reflected glory much more than her sister, and that was all right with Rowenna. Her sister enjoyed it, and Rowenna didn't care a fig one way or the other.

It was four days later that Mustard was again saddled and bridled and saddle-bagged. The chinky pins must still be gotten, and sooner or later she would be required to climb again to the cave.

Chin lifted and lips firmly clenched, she entered the cave and looked around. No sign of blood or any object that was not found in any of the many caves in northwest Arkansas. A sigh of relief. A nod of the head.

She left the cave and climbed onto the tall rock that had been used as a horse-boarding help. There was absolutely no sign that it had been so importantly used. Good. The woodland was efficient at cleaning up after itself.

Where the man had fallen, the leaves had blown into place, and there was no sign of blood or scuffle. Maybe it didn't really happen. If it was not for that horrid story in the paper, she might be able to forget it... but she knew she couldn't, actually. Not really and truly.

Something had happened in her life that required thinking about. There she had been, sneaking up the tree with her book... preparing for a lazy afternoon... and her head kept saying, *Chinky pin cave... chinky pin cave.*

Now, where was all that coming from? What had been the sense of it all? Of course, she had been feeling slightly guilty for reading instead of gathering the nuts, but that was not all of it.

The command within her head had been clear and insistent. Not a real voice like the one for the boy Samuel, but it was something she could not ignore, even for the pleasure of reading, for a third time, about her wonderful nurse hero who was so brave. About the girl who knew at an early age how to help when so many soldiers were wounded.

That nurse that kept insisting that the wounds must be kept clean. Hands must be washed, and knives from surgery must be sterilized… and that meant actually being boiled. Even more important than what she did, it seemed, was how it was done, and the first thing was cleanliness.

But Rowenna knew all that. Where did the voice in her head come from? Then came another strange thought. *Rowenna, I'm proud of you.*

Nothing new there. The whole world, it seemed, was proud of her, and she had done absolutely nothing to be proud of. She had just finally decided to get the nuts as she had been assigned and happened onto the kidnapping. She had only done what had to be done, and she was the only one to do it. Because she was there.

Yes, Rowenna, you did what had to be done, and you were the only one to do it. And something more… *You were chosen as the BEST one to do it.*

The best one? *Yes. You were strong, you had the horse, you knew where the cave was, you knew immediately where to take the baby and you had a valuable skill with the gun. Not only that, you were able to climb quickly into the tree rather than facing a more powerful gun on the ground.*

And today, on the hillside, she shook her head stubbornly. *No. What I did was just a sudden thought. I just decided to do it without thinking.*

Yes, Rowenna, and that is the reason you were the best one to do this.

Rowenna plunked down on top of the tall stone, drew her legs up under her longer skirt and folded her arms on her knees. Leaning her head forward, she breathed deeply and considered her thoughts. The comforting weight of the gun pulled her skirt aside a bit, but she hardly noticed it.

It took twenty minutes of thought for the voice to convince her that what happened was not a coincidence or an accidental collision of events. *Face it, Rowenna. You were sent. Someone knew where you were, and you were sent BECAUSE YOU WOULD GO!*

Finally, nodding agreement, she slipped down from the rock at serious risk to her modesty once more, but there was no one around to see but the squirrels. Hey, how about taking two or three of them home when she took the nuts?

Nodding again, she decided she would gather the nuts first and make sure she wouldn't need the bullets for any other purpose. The tiny chestnuts were so thick under the massive tree that in no time she had the bags full. Slipping quietly among the trees, she sighted in on the speedy animals with the fluffy tails.

Four would be plenty for a batch of dumplings, and her ma made the very best of those flavorful, doughy morsels. That would be supper for tomorrow, and then she would bring Mustard back to Granddad. She still had thinking to do, and maybe her hilltop home would help her make sense of what had just happened.

There was still the new book about Clara Barton. She lived almost a hundred years ago, and she did a really important thing by gathering people together into something called the Red Cross. It was going to be very exciting to read, but she couldn't read it yet. Not yet. There was still thinking to be done.

It was time to take Mustard back to Granddad, and maybe he could help her think. "Granddad, it is embarrassing to be praised for something I didn't do. I was NOT brave, and if I could have gotten away, I would never have shot the man."

Granddad nodded. "Let's go over to the Big Three and get ice cream. I think it's strawberry today. Could you stand that?"

She grinned in appreciation of his attempts of humor. Granddad did try.

There were chunks of the tasty fruit embedded in the frozen delicacy, and they ate in silent appreciation. It never lasted long, but it was good for producing thoughts.

"My dear, you do not really know what you did. Maybe it is embarrassing to you now, but today, a lot of people know of you who didn't know you last week. We do not see the future, and there may be a reason why this knowledge is important and why events happened this way. Think about it. Of all the caves that could have been used, the kidnappers chose the chinky pin cave, even though others were much handier to Ridge Road. Think about that."

She did. Now was the time to tell him something important. "Granddad, I want to be a nurse like Florence Nightingale. I don't know how to do it, but I want to learn everything that she knew and read about everything that she did. If I hadn't read her book, I wouldn't have known to tie up the woman's bleeding leg."

The old man nodded. "But here is the thing… you DID read the book. You did know what to do. But now, I doubt there is a school anywhere in Arkansas to teach what you want to know. The schools with that knowledge will be in the big cities where there are more people who need them."

"I know, Granddad. What I want now is the books they use in the schools. I can learn without a teacher, and maybe… well, that is exactly what I want. Do you think I can get it?"

"I don't know, but we'll work on it."

THE SIGNBOARD

To back up a bit.

In the days when the pair consisting of Rowenna and Wally were ten and eleven-and-a-half and looking for fun, the new, young preacher, Reverend Harvey Clemmons, had constructed a sign board out on the church lawn that he called a 'marquee'. With a clever positioning of some panels, he was able to slide needed letters along in the 'pocket' to leave statements that… he hoped… would set the town's people to thinking.

It was rather a time-consuming job, positioning the wooden letter shapes, and it was not one of the preacher's favorite duties, so he had assigned it to Wally, knowing his cousin would find a way to help.

So, at least once a week, the girl would be standing with the box of black-painted wooden letters. She would be sorting through the pile for the next letter as Wally positioned them and slid them into place.

Somehow, though they became older, there had never been a reason to give up the job, so the two usually found time to do it together. It took some planning, though.

Rowenna was now set about learning the rudiments of sewing… or at least how to repair a split-out seam and to sew on a button. Wally, now going on fifteen, was regularly employed by the WM. It was his special duty to climb to the various mountain cabins where there were suppliers of the eggs, cheese and butter for the store. That little chore kept him on the road, so to speak, and that was why he was gone when Nathan was enlisted to help Rowenna in the kidnap caper.

In addition to the dairy products, there were often jellies sent to the store for credit that would be placed against their purchases of flour and other items that could not be grown. This loaded Wally's saddle bags both ways, but the horses were accustomed to the mountains and climbed like mountain goats.

Wally really liked the job and felt lucky that he was selected. Eventually he would be working in the store building, selling and stocking shelves, and that was considered a really good job. The WM was about the best-paying job for boys and young men in the whole town of Wishbone.

Wally knew that Nathan, whose family owned the WM, did not really like that business but wanted to be a pharmacist... whatever that was. It seemed that the barber shop sold about all the stuff like that that anybody would need. So why do all that learning when a good job with his family was his already? But that was not Wally's problem.

He still liked the church sign. It was continuously interesting to see what Preacher Clemmons would think of next. Some of the sentences had so many words that the letters had to be snugged close to get them all on... like 'Life has many choices but eternity has only two. Which is yours?'

Then there was 'Life is shorter than you think,' 'Making excuses doesn't change the truth,' 'Never give the devil a ride. He likes to drive,' and 'Look not behind or ahead, but within.'

And there was Wally's personal favorite, 'Never throw dirt, you only lose ground.'

Once and a while he picked something from the Bible. This was one of those times. Rowenna had waited until Wally was back from the mountains, and she stood by the sign with the box of letters. When Wally called for a letter, she sorted it out while he worked the former one into place.

This was a medium-short one. 'The eyes of the Lord are in every place.' The girl set the box on the ground and stood back. Trembles and shivers ran down her arms as her mind pictured a girl sitting on a limb with a book she intended to read. She saw the girl contentedly jiggling the swing rope for the dog.

It struck her like a thunderbolt of new knowledge, but it was something she had always known. God saw her sitting there, and he wanted her to do a little chore for him. If it had not been for the chinky pins, it might have been hard to leave the book and go... but THERE WAS the chinky pins! There should be NO accidental coincidences for those who belong to God. That was what Granddad was trying to say.

Wally was watching. "Uh... what's the matter?"

"Nothing. No, that's not right. It's something. The eye of the Lord is in EVERY place."

"Uh... yes. We always knew that."

The girl shook her head. "No, I didn't. I never thought of it, but he saw me on the limb and sent an angel with a message to me. The angel had a bit of a time getting my attention. It's kind of scary, don't you think?"

Wally thought for a minute. "Row, I think it's supposed to be scary. Say... why do you think it was an angel in your head... and not God?"

The girl shook her head in puzzlement. Surely he knew why.

"It had to be an angel, because God has made so many of us he has given special duties to the angels... or they wouldn't have anything to do. Don't you remember? That's what they told us when we were little. It had to be an angel, because the message was to me out of all the people in the world. Not very many folks know where the chinky pin cave is, and most of the ones who do were busy... like you... and couldn't go. I was the one who would understand, and the message was specific about the cave."

Her cousin seemed doubtful, so she continued. "There was that important time when he told a human lady she would be the mother of his son. That message came by an angel."

"But Mary actually saw the angel."

"Sure. That message was too hard to believe without an angel standing there. I knew exactly what the message was. I just didn't know why, and I didn't want to go."

"You're probably right." And he continued with the letter placements.

The girl stood looking at the sign, and the boy continued. "Maybe it is a little scary to be told to do something immediately. I hope if I get a message from an angel, it will be to stay at the WM for years and years."

But that was not to be.

WHEN ROWENNA WAS FOURTEEN

Not a great lot was made of birthdays in Arkansas in 1910. It meant you were a year older and possibly would be moved up to a higher grade of the chores that kept the family going. On top of that, you had one of those birthdays every year, so what was the big thing?

Rowenna turned fourteen in the hilltop house with her parents, and there was very little to do. Most of her siblings had gone, and there was time for her to be lazy. Jadeen had the job at the Wishbone Cryer, and the two next older brothers were lumberjacks by the week. They only came home long enough to leave their dirty clothes and enjoy home cooking. Laverne lived over in Eureka, and the others were sprinkled over Wishbone, Eureka, Bentonville and Fayetteville. So there was practically nothing left to do.

Past helping with the washing, tossing hay to the horses and a small amount of cooking, Rowenna had time to read.

The Clara Barton book was absolutely marvelous. She was so clever and smart and saw the need to organize nursing… and she seemed to know how it was done. That was just about all Rowenna could think of any more.

There had to be a way for her to learn more, but there were certainly no schools in Arkansas that taught nurses how to be nurses. It seemed that both Florence Nightingale and Clara Barton taught themselves… or… what?

Maybe Granddad had ideas. There was one other little fall chore that she was required to do, and after that she'd see what he had to say.

That chore was gathering the fall muscadines. The deep purple, thick-skinned native grapes grew wild if left alone… or on special trees if the small vines were gathered and re-set.

Someone before her had set the vines into a grove of trees about a quarter mile from the house, and all it took to harvest them was a pail and the ability to climb. It wasn't an easy climb… like into the oak. This was a tough climb through thick vines.

Not only that, the vines seemed to hug the tree and attach themselves firmly, but one could not count on that. They could let loose at any minute and a whole two or three yards of vine could separate from the tree, and you could find yourself sitting on the ground… or maybe laying on the ground.

Climbing was not the problem with Rowenna… it was the new longer skirts. She needed a couple of extra hands to manage the skirts and two more hands for the limbs. In past years, her next older brothers performed this little duty, and last year, there was Jadeen, who could not climb very well but could go for help if needed.

She had made a decision that next year, she would shed the skirt and wear a pair of her brothers' outgrown overalls. The muscadines must be gathered at all costs, because the jam was such a favorite with the family.

So… with a bucket attached to her waist with a belt, she held to branches as her feet found the footholds. Great clusters of the tangy-sweet fruit were clipped from the vine and put in her bucket. The timing for this job must be precise… wedged between the cooler fall weather needed to sweeten the fruit and the appetites of migrating birds who loved them.

So she had time to think. She'd always loved to read, and she had read most everything she could get her hands on… but why the nursing book? Could the angel who brought the message have something to do with it? It was a book that Mama had to order special. That was unusual. And it was a book that was advertised in the back of the Florence Nightingale book.

Rowenna was close enough to the sky to use a little imagination. Looking up through the top limbs of the tree, she said, "Angel…? Are you up there? If you had anything to do with getting me that book, maybe you can help with something else."

As the sound of her voice echoed in her ears, she had to grin at the foolishness of it all. A fourteen-year-old girl hanging onto a muscadine vine… in a tree… on an Arkansas hillside… attempting to talk with an angel. Ridiculous! Granddad would get a charge out of that if she dared to tell him.

Having nothing else to do except clip the grape clusters from the vines, she pretended the angel responded, asking her what she needed help with.

Hmmmm, how could she put this…?

"Angel, if it would be all right with you… and your Boss, of course… I would like the study books that nurses work from when they get to go to school. It seems like you might know me, and if you do, you know that I had no trouble studying by myself at school and I made good grades. Does that help any…?"

Somehow the idea did not seem so stupid now. She popped a couple of the grapes into her mouth and leaned against the limb. Her bucket was full, and she was going to have to let it down to the ground. This was where Jadeen was a help, but she had no Jadeen. Holding to the rope and working the pail carefully in and out of the limbs, she felt the bucket touch the ground below, and she dropped the rope after it.

Now to climb down backward, looking for the footholds without Jadeen to tell her if she was close. She kept stepping on a part of her skirt. This was clearly not going to work. She could kill herself out here, and no one would ever know!

Loosing one hand, she gathered a handful of skirt and pettislip and lifted it to her mouth, firmly clutching in between her teeth. Then a rattle sounded through the limbs below her.

Oh…! There went the 22mm! Did little guns break? Maybe the thick limbs broke the fall. Maybe it would get caught on the way down.

"Angel? Did you see that? I just can't let that gun be broke. Granddad said I must never be without it in the woods."

Holding her skirt in her mouth, she descended as quickly as was safe. There, about 3 feet from the ground, the little gun was hanging, its barrel having slipped into a tangle of vines. Rowenna giggled with relief.

"Thank you, Angel. Thank you! Thank you! Thank you!" She forced herself not to add, "Don't go away, Angel. I'm sure to need you again." That, she decided, would be taking more liberty than she deserved.

And over in the Thimble and Spools, a conference had been going on for several days... what to do about Rowenna's gun and her dress pocket. There was, of course, no way the current situation could be permitted to continue. It was just not done by young ladies.

But there was the fact that if she had not had the gun... and done what she did, she would now be dead. Nathan had been very clear about that.

"How about a special little holster like the men use? Could we make something like that?" Cecelia was doubtful, but the conversation must start somewhere.

"Uh... no. I don't think she would even wear it if we made it. Remember, she didn't ask for help, so we have to be careful."

"Yes... but what it does to her pocket... we must...."

"And now everyone in five counties knows that she carries a...."

"I know. We have to keep thinking."

"How about a pocket in her pettislip?"

"Well, she would have to wear a thicker fabric, and she wouldn't like that."

"But she might have to...."

"Think, Georgiana, has Rowenna ever done what we wanted her to do unless she wanted to do it?"

"No, but... Well..." And the trio of loving ladies sighed a collective sigh of frustration.

"Maybe... think on this. If she had a small holster that just fit the little gun and a way to fasten it to her waist, maybe she would wear it under her skirt and over her pettislip. I've heard of courting ladies carrying their 'mad money' that way in case they got angry with their partner and had to hire a way to get themselves home."

The other two ladies brightened. Maybe they could deal with this idea. If they could remember the size of the gun... really about the size of her hand. And some fabric, soft like broadcloth, which might not last long, but they could make her several.

Aunt Sophrenia put action to her words and hauled out an outdated copy of the Cryer, carefully hoarded for such purposes as this. With the scissors, she snipped out a shape and proceeded to trim it as each of the ladies thought it should be.

Now, for the belt. The girl was rather small, so that would be no problem.

Rowenna's angel might have enjoyed a smile at the industriousness of the three ladies… if angels actually smile at the unexplainable things humans do… and continue to think it was their own idea.

Rowenna backed carefully down the height of the muscadine tree and stepped to the solid earth of the Arkansas mountain. She sighed with satisfaction. There were seven one-gallon buckets of the grapes setting in the cart, and when she set the last one in the cart, it would hold no more. Eight gallons was the goal.

Pocketing her gun, she picked up the tongue of the wagon and headed for her house. She'd find overalls for her next trip. Tomorrow, she promised herself, she would go see Granddad. She had a whole armful of questions she would ask him.

But that was not to be.

TROUBLE IN EUREKA SPRINGS

It seemed like when stupid little old contagious diseases decided to strike a certain town, they did a good job of it. When diphtheria stuck Wishbone a decade ago, it did a painful number on the little ones and just about decimated the fledgling school system.

At least half the seats were made empty… with five and six-year-olds gone before it was even decided there was something to worry about. Doctors were either nonexistent or too far away to reach, so the people did what they could. Most residents had a sore throat sometime during the winter, and the little ones could not explain to the 'wise' grownups that what they had was more than a sore throat… until they had no breath to speak.

The school board, with 47 students from the farms sprinkled about on the hillsides, quietly removed 23 of the little desks and rearranged the pattern of those remaining.

But now the school had two rooms and a general average of 70 students total, and it was not Wishbone this time that was in the center of the epidemic storm. It was the much larger town two hollows over to the west.

Eureka Springs was attacked with the Hard Red Measles... so named to differentiate them from the onset of the milder chicken pox and the 'roseola' rash that attacked mostly small children with a high temperature, then a rash of only several days.

By the time the first flush of Eureka's patients were broken out, attention was paid, and immediately the local authorities gave it a second look. Most of the new patients were young and strong and had jobs. This was definitely not a young childhood outbreak and quickly took on the well-known name of Hard Red Measles... the kind that that laid the patient low for two and a half weeks and left them weak as a kitten for another month. If they lived.

For some of a more delicate physical stature, it could be fatal, and for those women who were pregnant, it could and often did leave a blind child to cope with the aftermath.

For those only weeks along in their pregnancy, the disease often caused a miscarriage... which was considered a blessing, all things considered.

So the Hard Red Measles attacked the small Arkansas town of Eureka Springs. The first action was to shut out outsiders, and the second was to issue a thermometer to any household not having one. Young men who were available and physically able were set about to find every mountain cabin and equip the inhabitants with information and a thermometer. They were told that a temperature meant quarantine for the whole family for at least a week and that the affected person must wear a bandana over their face for that period of time.

Places of business did not trust the home-applied thermometer for their employees but required their own alcohol-dipped instrument applied to everyone as they entered the door. They also hoped their few remaining customers would be as astute.

The actors in the local theaters were no different. That was when it was discovered that Laverne Moffat, the actress who was so skillful at dying on the stage, now stood a chance of having acquired the possibly fatal disease.

She was sent home with a thermometer and not invited back until the temperature was normal. Maybe tomorrow… but that was not to be.

As a special, personal favor to a valued actress, a boy on a pony was sent to the Moffat home in Wishbone with the command to come and get their daughter, who could not be left alone in her apartment.

It was at this moment that Rowenna, satisfied and pleased after her discussion with the angel, who was surely watching over her, was pulling her last cart of muscadines up the hill to her home.

She saw the boy with the pony as he rode away from her house. Hmmm, something important must have happened that they needed her pa. The delivered note was on its third reading as she entered the house.

"Bernard, you gotta go over to Eureka and get that girl. The hard measles gonna put her down… and her over there alone. Good chance she wouldn't… you gotta go…."

Pa was nodding agreement as he clearly saw his duty. He was running through his mind which horse to put to the buggy that could make the quickest trip when Jadeen, home at the time, stared with open-mouthed horror.

"Pa! You can't bring her here! I ain't had the hard measles, and I'd have to stay home for a month, and I'd lose my job for sure. Besides that, we got no measles here, and the whole town'll be mad if we bring it to 'em."

Pa and Ma listened, knowing she spoke with a degree of sense. "But, Jadeen, your sister is sick. Of course she'll be coming home. We'll just put her…."

"NO, MA! We can't have her nowhere here. Get someone over there to take care of her!"

"Now, think about it, Jadeen. In an epidemic, there ain't those standin' around ready to take care of…."

"WAIT!" she screamed. "I know what to do! Send Rowenna over there to take care of her. She's done had those… remember how you sent her down to Thimbles so Laverne and I wouldn't get it?"

Hmmm. Well, that was a thought. A possibility. Rowenna stared from one parent to the other and then toward her sister, who was livid with fear and screaming. Somehow, however this came out, Rowenna knew she was going to be affected. The only other choice would be to send Laverne down to Thimbles, and then the town would be sure enough mad, as that establishment was located almost at the center of town.

And Wishbone had no doctor. There were several residents who could be counted to give the best advice they could, effective or not. One was Ma.

Rowenna, barely fourteen, stared at her family members and had no words. Her mind played a few scenes before her eyes. A girl hidden in the tree with a small gun… a sign in the church yard: 'The eye of the Lord is in every place'… Granddad's words, 'You were the only one who could do what you did,' and the recent view of the tree branches that had separated her from the angel who must certainly have been listening. Maybe.

Her three family members turned toward her, her ma with her hand over her mouth in her best 'thinking' expression.

"Well… she HAS had the measles, and she doesn't have a job. She knew to tie a bandage on that woman's leg, and they say that likely saved her life. We could…."

Jadeen brightened considerably. "I'll help 'er pack, Ma. She could take eggs and things Laverne would need, and maybe… there's the aspirins we just bought. And Pa could take her… and…."

One could say this for Jadeen… she was quite the little planner. The thing was, someone had to do it, and she seemed to have come up with something that would work. Not only that, there was no time to spare, because Laverne was stuck in that other town sick… and totally alone.

Something had to be done immediately, and Rowenna had the same sensation she had while hiding behind the tree trunk doing the only thing she saw to do.

She hardly had time to think until she was in the buggy riding behind the clipping hoof-steps of Peppersauce, so named for her mottled, reddish color. She was a young, light-footed pony with surprising endurance. Whichever way they looked at it, the pony must make the trip there and back, because Pa would not be permitted to even look at Laverne.

The buggy held hastily gathered supplies and preparations, and her head held instructions. "Soda and boric acid for the bumps, Rowenna. She MUSTN'T scratch, even if you have to tie up her hands. That makes those puss-filled sores that turn into scars. Keep washing her, and yourself, and don't you eat from the same dishes she does, even if you've washed 'em."

Ma thought a minute and repeated instructions. "Now, see you wash both you and her in that pink Lifebuoy soap to get clean and then in the green Palmolive so you don't chaff. You got all the Lysol I had, and you'll manage to get more if you need it. Eureka stores'll be stocked up. And then there's that Mrs. Stewart's Bluing that eases pain. Wash her bumps with that and powder her with cornstarch if they get to itchin', and remember...."

Pa finally clicked to Peppersauce to take off while Ma was still giving instructions... for the third time. They cleared the yard in a full gallop and headed for the gravel road that crossed the ridges. The road was a bit winding, but it avoided going down into a hollow and back up again. A lot of tiny towns appeared on the ridge, but Wishbone and Eureka were nestled down in a valley.

By sundown, Pa would get her there, and he would be coming home in the dark. Right now, he was leaning forward with the reins as though that way might help Peppersauce's speed. His pale blue eyes were as fierce as the golden eyes of a preying eagle. Number eleven child was in trouble, and he was taking number thirteen into the same epidemic. Surely....

And he tapped the lines against Peppersauce's smooth, rounded rear just to remind her he was in a hurry. Her dainty hooves clicked on the flint-rock gravel of the road, and her tail lifted out proudly. She knew she was a beautiful animal.

The tap-tap of the hooves soothed the girl. She sighed and watched the scenery go by... the purple stars of the fall asters blooming along the roadside and the brightness of the buttercups open for the last visits of the flocks of yellow butterflies.

'The eye of the Lord…" It would have to be a very big eye… or perhaps compound like the eyes that he gave to houseflies. The kind that can see forward and backward without turning.

Her mind finished the verse. "…in every place, beholding the evil and the good." So he saw Laverne, sick and not at home with her family. So interesting to Rowenna that she herself had been the only one of the later family members to have the hard measles, and thereby she was qualified to go tend to her sister.

The timing was good, actually, as her best friend, Jewelee, was spending her time with her nose in books, studying to take the test for a teaching certificate. She was determined to make the very best score so she would be ready when one of the two jobs in Wishbone became vacant. Until then, she would be the best qualified person to substitute when needed.

The sun was lowering when Pa turned Peppersauce into the road down into Eureka. There was almost no one on the streets. Pa was stopped and asked his business. He stated in a few words that he was dropping off help for his daughter. The guard took a look at Rowena's fourteen-year-old face and back to Pa with a question.

Pa shrugged and added, "This here's the Girl with the Gun. She knows what she's doin'."

"Oh! Oh, yes. Bring 'er on, but don't stop over. Get on out before dark."

And it was already getting dark in the small Arkansas town.

THE MONTH IN EUREKA SPRINGS

There were boxes and sacks to off-load. All of Rowenna's clothes, for a starter, and the disinfectants, along with a lot of towels, mostly old and well-worn. Ma also sent along a 'starter' box of food.

Following instructions from Ma, Rowenna refused to allow Pa to enter the house. "Don't be lettin' 'im in to see her. After all this trouble, he don't need to be bringin' none of it back with him."

So Pa stacked the plunder by the door, and Rowenna bravely picked everything up and set it into the tiny parlor.

Laverne had been phenomenally fortunate to get this little house so close to the center of town. It had been constructed long ago for someone's old ma who had gone on. Two tiny rooms with hardly a kitchen at all. No matter... Rowenna didn't plan to do much cooking. She definitely had other plans.

The tiny cabin, however, had running water just outside the door. Piped down from a spring farther up the hill, she had only to turn the tap and fill her buckets, dump in the disinfectant and pick up the scrub cloths. Ma had insisted she roll up the small rug and cover the floor boards with Lysol disinfectant water.

Laverne was in the small bedroom under a pile of covers. Chills but no fever at this minute. Perfectly normal. Her worst problem right now was that she was extremely angry with the world in general, and her sister was part of it.

"What're you supposed to do? I thought Pa was coming after me."

"Wishbone didn't want you over there, and most of it was comin' from Jadeen. So I was assigned to put up with you for a month or maybe more. I agree... it'll be no picnic for either of us. Quick as I get through with the floors, you're getting a bath. Ma said. Either you do it or I do it, and it will be every day. She says it will help with the itch and hurry up the healing. I had it when I was too little to remember anything except the smell of the Lysol and the itch."

"I don't feel like a bath. I'm freezing."

"I'll make a fire, but between the two of us, I think I may be the strongest, and you WILL take a bath. Either that, or I will walk home and leave you alone. If I start first thing early in the morning, I can make it home just after dark."

With that firm promise to set the ground rules, she sopped up the liquid from the flooded floor. Then she remembered something else from her own bout with the illness. Measles stink in their own unique way. Sort of a gagging stink. So her sister was sure to be breaking out this very minute. Ma said to change the sheets every day to avoid reinfecting her.

This was not going to be a picnic. Her only pleasure was that Eureka had a library, and it was only a few steps away. When she got all of the 'have to's' done, she'd sneak out and do a little research on her own plans.

She shook her head to drive out the problems Ma said might occur. Her sister was also strong-minded and not in charge. She couldn't... and wouldn't let messy things happen... could she...? Like the many cloths Ma sent for when the patient could not stand up to take care of her personal necessities.

So with the small house now reeking with cleanliness, she started the next meal. Her sister warned that she did not want anything, but Rowenna did... and she wasn't sick. She'd worked up quite an appetite. Potato soup to start with. With lots of onions to drown out some of the disinfectant smell.

Rowenna was not much of a cook but was good with potato soup. Laverne turned away and gagged. Rowenna mashed potato chunks in the broth and administered six tiny bites before the patient burst into a flood of tears and refused to open her mouth. Oh, well, she could afford to lose a pound or two.

For herself, Rowenna fried a slice of salt pork and a pair of eggs. That and the soup, with crackers, went perfectly. Now for a place to sleep.

The floor boards were still damp, so she stretched the ironing board between two chairs and scooted them against the wall. It would have to do. It did nicely until 2:00. An ear-bursting shriek issued from the bedroom, and a hysterical voice screamed, "FIRE! I'm on FIRE!"

The candle...? Rowenna rolled out of bed and dashed to her side.

Wild-eyed, her patient had thrashed her covers off the bed and was throwing her head back on the pillow. Holding the candle closer, Rowenna saw the fiery-red patches on her sides and inner thighs. Grabbing the water pail, she headed for the yard. Cold water, Ma had said. Face and neck. Maybe stomach. Ma ought to know... she'd gone through this with eight others.

Sponging her face was not easy with Laverne's arms lashing out to push her away. Keep at it... Ma had warned, so Rowenna did. Finally the patient quieted, exhausted, and allowed herself to be re-covered with a quilt. Rowenna pulled a kitchen stool into the room and watched her until morning. Groans and bouts of restlessness. Then a different smell.

What had happened was what Ma had warned about. She would have to be washed where no eighteen-year-old girl wanted to be washed, but she seemed not to realize anything was happening. Ma had said the sheet would have to be changed and had instructed how to do it… in the final minutes before she left Wishbone. "Make half the bed and roll her over. Then finish."

"Then you'll have to pin on a… uh, pad…?"

Wide-eyed, Rowenna had whispered, "A diaper… Ma…?"

Ma had continued to fill the grocery box but nodded, rapidly.

In the dim light of dawn, she changed the sheets, and her sister had no knowledge of being moved. Now for the protecting pad. How degrading. Fortunately her patient seemed to have no knowledge….

Rowenna wadded the soiled sheets and put them outside the door. Ma had said, "See you boil them sheets for fifteen minutes…."

Bringing in another pail of water, Rowenna stoked the small stove and set the pail on to heat. Just as well get started. Laverne finally opened her eyes and looked around but didn't seem to understand she must not throw off her quilts. The windows were shaded to protect her eyes, so her nurse had to squint to see what she had to do. "Shh…" she chided, finger to lips.

When the wash pail began to steam, she crammed in the sheets, pouring in most of the Lysol. She'd have to manage to get more tomorrow. Struggling to hold her eyes open, she knew she had to have tea… or something. Would it be safe to heat the tea on the same stove as the boiling sheets…?

Of course. What was she thinking? She'd already had these terrible measles, and the aunts had taken care of her. She rinsed off a pair of eggs and eased them into the tea water. Why waste heat?

Ma had sent leftover biscuits, which Rowenna toasted and buttered heavily. Breakfast was served.

Her patient was groaning but seemed not to hear words. No use trying to feed her anything unless she could swallow. Would it be possible to encourage swallowing…? If there was only someone to ask. So many questions. She felt as though she was tossed into strange water with her arms strapped to her side. Sinking. Helpless. Totally hopeless. She could not do this, and that was clear.

Bending over her eggs and toast, she felt the tears coming. Tears of pity. She could not do this, and they had no right to make her. It should have been Ma... not her. Head leaned forward on her arms, she sobbed and sniffled.

Then she heard her sister call... "Ma...? Are you there, Ma...?"

Leaving the eggs, she dashed to the bedroom. Laverne was looking at her as though she actually knew her. Forcing brightness, she greeted, "Good morning. How do you feel?"

"I'm sick. Where's Ma?"

Think quick. "She isn't here right now, but she wanted you to drink tea, and I have it ready."

"No, please... I'm too sick."

"That's why you have to have tea. You have to get well, and if you don't have liquid when you have a fever, you get a lot worse." She remembered that from her Florence Nightingale book.

She tried to help her sit and lean back on the pillow, but she was just not quite strong enough. Tipping her shoulders forward, she elevated her enough to... maybe... sip tea.

With the first swallow, her patient screamed with pain. "My throat's been cut! It hurts so bad! Is there blood...?"

Rowenna drew in her breath and held it. Ma said nothing about this. Was her throat supposed to hurt... that was in diphtheria, wasn't it? She couldn't have that... could she? The tea was barely warm, so it couldn't be that.

Bringing a spoon, she dipped up a few drops and coaxed cooperation. Tipping the liquid in her mouth, most of it, maybe, went down. Try again. A few more drops. At this rate it was going to take a long time so she better get going. One after the other... and then another. Till about a half a cup of the tepid tea was gone. Laverne's tears were sliding down her face just about as fast as Rowenna was putting tea in her mouth. She needed something to numb her throat. What...?

WILLOW BARK? Could she still get it? It used to be available until aspirins came on the market, and then only the old folks had it. The aunts had it, but that was miles away. The closest store was... where...?

The sun was up, and the store, wherever it was, would be open by the time she got herself ready. She'd just have to leave her sister; there was no other way. She'd sneak out quietly. Laverne likely couldn't get up, anyway.

Easing her sister back down in the bed, she pulled up the covers and tiptoed out. Shaking the wrinkles from her skirt and pulling a bonnet on her uncombed hair, she slipped out and ran down the small hill to Main Street.

Store, store, where are you? Barber shop was just a short way, and a man went in. Running toward him, she begged, "Wait, please. I need help." He waited.

Yes, he could help. It happened he still had a few customers who wanted that old-fashioned pain reliever, but the barber had something else, in addition. There was the liquid to gargle for sore throats, and if she was too sick to gargle, a few drops in a spoon and put in her mouth would ease her throat. Maybe.

"Take both, my dear, and pay me later when she's well. You must hurry back to her."

Rowenna nodded and took the bottle and the package. Scurrying back up the hill, she slipped herself back in the cabin. No sound. Lifting the boiling sheets to the floor, she put on the teakettle again. Tipping the shavings of willow bark into a cup, she drew in a breath and waited. Which should she do first... the willow bark that she knew about... or the gargle that was recommend? She opened the bottle, and a strong aroma of peppermint and cinnamon filled the room, easily overpowering the Lysol.

Hmmmm, well, maybe the peppermint. She couldn't use much, he said, because it was mostly gargled and spit, and her patient likely couldn't spit. Teaspoon, then. Tipping a few drops in the spoon, Rowenna poured them down her own throat. They slid down nicely, and the peppermint flavor was very bracing. Decision made.

Peppermint first, and then the tea. Maybe she could get more than a half a cup of liquid down her. That was a MUST, according to her book. Fever burned up liquid in the blood, and then the blood could not... uh, what was it the book said? Something about the blood and what it did. Just couldn't remember. She needed the book.

Then a call from the bedroom. "Row...? Are you there?"

At least she seemed to be aware. Relieved sigh. Time for the throat medicine. "Coming...." she called.

Armed with the bottle and a spoon, she approached the bed.

"Take that away!" Her voice was as cracked and gravelly as a crow. It was almost possible to hear the pain.

"Can't. This is good stuff. Slipped out and bought it special for you."

"NO!"

"All right," Rowenna agreed as she set it aside while her patient watched... somewhat suspicious and totally unbelieving that this battle could be won so easily. These sisters had often locked heads, and Rowenna, though more than four years younger, mostly held her own quite well.

So now was the time for more demands. "And don't pin any more of those... things... on me. I'm getting up." Whereupon she flung her feet to the floor and pushed herself upright.

"Good!" encouraged her captor. "Try it."

Laverne jerked herself upright, and the room suddenly rearranged itself with the darkened window now on the ceiling. Not only that, the bedside rug was flinging itself toward her face. She lunged forward and found herself draped across the arms and shoulders of her sister.

Rowenna eased her back to the bed and impudently demanded, "Now what...?" With a degree of childish satisfaction, she saw the tears form, shining on her cheeks in the dim light.

Rowenna relented. "I'll make a bargain. I'll move it close to the bed on one condition, that being that you accept help and don't try it by yourself."

Staring into her sister's eyes, she firmly added, "Or else."

"Or else what?"

"Or else I leave it right where it spills until you get well enough to clean it up."

Laverne capitulated. She decided she would rather live to fight again. That problem taken care of, Rowenna approached with the spoon and the bottle of red liquid.

"No. My throat is too sore."

"Yes, you will, and when this is done, you are getting a bath. Once with the pink soap and once with the green soap, and a rinse with bluing. Just like Ma said. And it will be an all-over bath."

"No."

Rowenna paused, smiling, and put down the bottle. Walking toward the coat hook, she lifted off her fall wrap and picked up the outdoor lantern.

"What are you doing...?"

"I'm going home. If I start now, I'll be there by midnight if I take the cut-off path. When Ma wakes up, I'll tell her what happened, and she'll be over here. Of course, I was planning to be as gentle as I could be, but I have an idea of how Ma will be if she has to come over here."

The sisters stared at each other and might still be staring, but Laverne suddenly gagged and heaved, bringing up nothing because she had eaten nothing. She convulsed and gagged again, head flinging back on the pillow, being supported by strong, fourteen-year-old arms.

In the course of the attack, Rowenna felt the fever in her sister's underarms and forehead. The nurse in her shivered with tension... all was not well. Easing her back on the pillow, she sat on the bed and opened the bottle, pouring a little of the red liquid into the spoon.

Steadying the shivering chin with her hand, she tipped the spoon in her mouth. Not enough to strangle, but enough to drain to her throat. The strong aroma of cinnamon and peppermint filled the room. With the hand against her chin, she felt the swallow... without the scream.

After waiting a quiet minute for the numbness to set in, she tipped in another half-teaspoon full. Enough... Now for the willow tea that would actually do some good. The tea would have a small effect on the fever, and the bath would follow. Laverne might be stubborn, but she knew her sister was right about Ma, and she also knew when she was done in.

Fifteen minutes later, the tea was steeped and ready. Dipping it up with a soup spoon, Rowenna held a cloth against her sister's chin and slowly drizzled it back. After about the fourth spoonful, Laverne reached for the cup. After about half, Rowenna retrieved the cup. She didn't want to risk it being heaved up onto the quilt. Again.

The tea was quite effective with pain and fever. Eyes drooping, she settled back on the pillow, and Rowenna snugged the quilt around her chin. The first of the fever must be allowed to rise (according to Clara Barton's book). Then, when it broke, she would give the bath, and she didn't expect any trouble from the patient.

Now what...? Real food for the nurse... that's what! She'd had nothing but what she'd snatched up while standing. That had to stop.

Checking that her patient was actually asleep, she crept out. The market would be close, and she could really hurry. A roasting chicken if they had one, and she would boil it until the broth was thick. That would do for Laverne at first.... just to see how it went. Maybe an orange if there were any. The WM didn't regularly keep oranges except special order or the Christmas season. The A&P here in Eureka was a lot bigger.

Armed with the chicken... really big... and three oranges... thin-skinned and seeming quite ripe, she left on a run. The aunts would be embarrassed if they saw her, but they weren't there. When she had been sick, there were three of them, and there was only one of her... unfortunately.

Just as she opened the door, her mind saw the marquee sign, "The eye of the Lord is in every place..." Startled, she looked around, but she was alone. She turned the door knob and told herself, *If the eyes of the Lord are on me, then he has instructed my angel to help. So I'm really not alone. It is me and the angel.* She nodded, liking the way that sounded. *Say, Angel, don't you ever think of leaving me, even for a minute. You see how cranky my sister can get when she's not doing what she wants to do.*

The aroma of the stewing chicken filled every corner of the room. It smelled wonderful, and Rowenna was certain she could eat every scrap... even the bones. She had just dipped off a half a cup of broth to be cooling when she heard from her patient.

"ROW...? Hey, Row, come help me stand up." She'd suffer the help rather than the upset chamber pot.

That necessity taken care of, a few drops of the red stuff to numb her sore throat, then the broth. Taking the lamp close to the bed, Rowenna could see that her sister was completely covered with red whelps. She mustn't be allowed to see a mirror, or she might decide life was not worth living. She looked decidedly terrible.

The patient managed almost a cup of broth. Wonderful! Juice later. First the pink and green soap and then the blue rinse. Rowenna could see the firm chin and tight lips registering pain... but no sound. Well, almost no sound. The bath completely exhausted her... so unlike the energetic and fidgety sister she always was.

Bath finished and sister dozing, Rowenna sat on the kitchen stool beside the bed and watched. She felt her whole insides filled with sympathy. Illness was so overwhelming. That must have been what Florence Nightingale felt. She had been from a well-to-do family who had plenty of money, and they were not so happy for their daughter to spend her life with sick and dying, especially on the battlefield of the Crimean War... yet!

Rowenna wondered... what would happen if she insisted on being a nurse? What would her parents say?

And while she thought of this, her sister, Jadeen, who worked for the Wishbone Cryer, was pushing things along. There was one way to spread the word about ANYTHING, and that was in the Classified Column of the paper. Along with what was being bought and sold came items of interest like birthday parties, a moving sale, and an award received by a school child.

The Classifieds often read this way:

CLASSIFIED ADVERTISTMENTS

Butcher hogs. Clive Buford on Echo Mountain off Robin Lane. Just follow your nose. Home most afternoons.

Milking short-horn bulls up for stud. First come, first served. Musgrave dairy.

Pattie's Candies has fresh pecan sandies. Bag or box. Also chocolate roses in foil.

And under these informative entries came Jadeen's contribution.

IMPORTANT NOTICE: My sister (remember The Girl with the Gun?) is now in Eureka. She is taking care of our sister with a bad case of hard measles. This notice is to inform Wishbone that I have not been exposed in any way to the measles, and if you see me around, you have no fear. The Girl with the Gun is taking care of everything about fifteen miles away.
And below this bit of information, the notices continued.

For all who left mending at my shop, everything is ready to be picked up. Bring cash, take finished clothing. The Hole-Mender. If you left something with me, then you know where I am.

Your horse tossed a shoe? I can get to the foot of the problem. Come in, and be sure to bring the horse. Jake's Smithing and Iron Shaping - quarter mile down Lost Horse Road.

This week's church sign: "If I hadn't wanted you, I wouldn't have made you. GOD." Come on Sunday and see what he wants with you.

And so on. For pennies per word, you could say anything in the Classifieds that wasn't illegal or openly offensive.

Rowenna had no idea she was being monitored, city-wide, during her absence. Likely it was a good thing she didn't know, as she had her hands full with her other sister.

Excited with her success over the chicken broth, she decided some soft-cooked rice pushed through the grater might work. Rice was easy to digest, and she could soften it with broth and flavor it with butter. This food thing could be a problem. Ma had given no ideas.

She needed a book from the library, but she dare not go. Something... almost anything... to read. Looking around in the library, however, and leaving her patient would be too risky. At least now. Maybe later.

All of Wishbone now knew exactly where Rowenna was and that included Eureka and other small hamlets. Nathan Wilkinson, among his other duties, scanned the Classifieds to know what was going on. The WM being one of the town's largest establishments, and the one seen regularly by the most people, made it a natural source of information.

Ah, there was Wally's cousin. And Nathan's mind reviewed the strange and sudden experience with her on the mountain and the surprise she had given him. He had thought that she might be injured or worse and that it would likely be a rescue, but he had found the battle over with her the victor.

Nathan had gone to school with the older sisters, Jadeen and Laverne, and he knew everyone in the tiny school. Being over two years older than Wally, they were not so much in the same group, but when he was hired by the WM, they became well-acquainted.

Of course, if Wally had not been in the mountains on delivery, it would likely have been he who was sent to help her. Possibly best that it worked out like it did, because Wally was younger and smaller, and it was quite unlikely that he could have managed to bring the woman back. It had been all Nathan could do, even with his greater strength, to manage to hold the woman and guide the horse... and hurry!

Possibly the hurrying was not all that necessary as Rowenna had already administered first aid, though how she knew what to do was unexpected. And there she was... sent to another town to take care of her sister through the hard measles. There must be more to her than he had thought.

He clearly remembered reaching up and picking her off the snaggy limbs of the tree as she tried to manage her skirts. Certainly Wally could not have done that. He was not tall enough, for one thing.

And he had held her upright during the fast and silent gallop back to town. He could still remember how she felt next to him... so trusting and so trembly after her ordeal. Understandably so. Shooting to scare away a bobcat or a snake was a long way from actually aiming to injure a human. What must have been going through her mind?

And he had not been aware at the time that she carried a gun. Of course, Wally was armed. It was absolutely necessary up in the mountains where he delivered groceries, but a girl…?

And her sister was calling her The Girl with the Gun, and the whole area knew who it was without calling her name. He'd thought about her a number of times since then but assumed to himself that her welfare was none of his business. She was, after all, almost five years younger than his almost nineteen years.

For some reason she kept coming into his mind. There was her bravery, skill and quick presence of mind. It was a bit confusing to remember that she was no longer a skinny little tag-along but someone to be accepted as a real person.

One thing about that little rescue incident: it gave him something to think on while he was stacking cans on grocery shelves for others to take down. And accepting money and paying bills, as these had also become his job.

Wally had a lot more to think of than his cousin's activities, though he was more than glad that she knew where to get help when he was not available. And there was the marquee sign. He thought of her with a small sigh as he sorted out his own next letter to copy the chosen remark. She had been so very handy all his life he'd failed to consider her ever being gone!

And the ladies at the Thimbles and Spools read with horror that their protégé had been packed off to the next town without even testing their latest design of a modest gun holster.

"That Jadeen! How dare she tell the world where Rowenna is and that she carries a gun! Calling her The Girl with the Gun! Did you ever…!"

"If we'd known she was leaving, we could have hurried. It was all so sudden… like…."

"Reckon they sent 'er off quick as they heard. Fact is, someone had to be with Laverne, and the whole town'd been in an uproar if she was brought here."

"Could be she was too sick to move. 'Member how it was with Rowenna that first week? Sometimes with us bein' not sure she would live."

Cecelia nodded. "Yes, and me not bein' sure we could handle someone already eighteen like Laverne. That'd be harder'n that baby was."

"Wish't we could'a seen how it hung so we'd know how to adjust it."

"When they sayin' she'll be back?"

"Don't say, but it'll be a month, for certain. Two weeks after the fever was what we always thought."

"One good thing is she'll have that gun with her, and she'll be safe over there all by herself."

Georgiana pointed out, "I'm thinkin' Eureka is fairly safe... and her living almost down on Main Street. Wonder where she caught the measles?"

"Likely someone who came to see her 'die' in one of her plays. I didn't figger no good would'a come of that actin'."

"But you know how stubborn them Moffats are."

"Yeah, and it don't help none on the youngens to be half Hopkins."

Aunt Sophrenia nodded to this and added her own concern. "I'm wonderin' if that girl knows about liquids and how important it is to get something down 'em, no matter how sick."

Neither of the other aunts had anything to add. They clearly remembered like it was yesterday how they had administered water with a medicine dropper when Rowenna seemed too sick to swallow.

And at that very moment, Rowenna was huddled on the high kitchen stool like a parrot on a perch, considering that very problem.

Laverne had to have water. She smiled faintly to think perhaps she could drizzle water into her ear... but, of course, that was just silly. The trouble with being sick is the nausea and the inability to get it down without it coming back up. There just had to be a way.

From what she read, after vomiting or blood loss, something had to replace the water. She had peeled and squeezed the juice from the oranges and tasted it. Delicious, but it was so tangy she had her doubts about it being swallowed. Maybe half water. Or maybe water mixed with willow tea.

Somehow it had to be done. *Ma had said it several times and she will ask when she sees me.* Uh, a thought! Seltzer water! Was there anything in it that would be bad for her patient? Maybe the barber had some. He was just about the best they had for a doctor when the town doctor was riding all over the mountainsides advising those with no ma to tell them what to do.

She sat there watching her sister in restless sleep. There was hardly a place where there was not a red bump or a red patch of skin. All over her face… and she was such a beautiful girl. She remembered when Laverne was about fourteen and she was ten that she heard comments about how Laverne took the good points from both sides of the family.

Rowenna nodded. *Yes, and left all the bad points for me…* but somehow it was just a thought for humor. She really didn't care if she was not pretty, and she couldn't see how being pretty would get her anything she could not get for herself.

Laverne seemed to be sleeping soundly. When she woke up, it would be the bath and an attempt to eat so, if she hurried, she could get to the barber shop for the seltzer and the library for something… anything… to read.

Bless that barber. He had small bottles of what he called 'fizz water.' She poked her head into the library. Only one person there.

"Come in! Come in! It's lonely in here," was the cheery invitation. A second look brought the comment, "Oh, you're the Girl with the Gun. The Cryer said you were here."

That Jadeen! Protecting her own hide, she was. "Really, I can't. I think Laverne's still contagious, but I'm desperate for something to read, if it's all right."

"Certainly! So let me see… do you like magazines? That stack by the door is throw-aways. If you like, you could take the whole dozen or so. Don't bring them back. That way you won't be nervous about spreading the measles. I've already had them, anyway."

Joyfully relieved, Rowenna grabbed up the tattered and dogeared magazines as if they were a life-raft on the ocean. Maybe they were. Dashing back to the little cabin, she was relieved to see that her sister still slept. Needed to wake her up and see how the liquid consumption went. Also get the bath over with before she, herself, got engrossed in the wonderful words printed on paper pages.

Entering the tiny bedroom, she sat on the bed and patted the quilt gently. Picking up her hand, she felt the skin. Cool. That meant the fever was down… at least at this moment. That also meant a fire needed to be built up so she wouldn't chill in the bath. The noise of fire building would be sure to wake her.

It did.

While the room warmed, Rowenna sat on the bed with a cup and a spoon and the half and half of orange juice and fizz. Laverne groaned wearily.

Rowenna tried to be cheerful. "Something different this time. Guaranteed to work without pain. It's coming by the spoonful… one right after another, and if this doesn't work, I'll have to go get Ma. I can't let you lay there and die. The world would never forgive me, because you're supposed to die before an audience."

Wonder of wonders… an attempt at a smile then a frown. Ouch… her whole face hurt.

Rowenna squared her shoulders bravely, dipped in the spoon and aimed for her sister's almost-open mouth. Tipping the liquid, it disappeared without a grimace. Hmmm, it was like the seltzer bubbles made the liquid lighter… easier to swallow. Her sister seemed to welcome it. Glory be! Maybe there was hope. It had been a long twelve days. She had lost at least ten pounds. That was not too bad, but it must be stopped… now.…

About two thirds of the cup of liquid disappeared somewhere. Rowenna stopped dipping, saying they mustn't get in a hurry and after the bath there would be more.

The cabin having heated comfortably, she began the bath. Her sister hated it maybe even more than Rowenna did, but she clearly could not bathe herself. Too exhausting. A slather of pink soap, a rinse and a slather of the green soap. Then a total rinse with the bluing. Dry thoroughly and a light dusting of boric acid for the itch and added healing.

She tried to notice the extent of the bumps without appearing to do so. Just as many. Maybe not so many of the new ones. Laverne did not seem to be tempted to scratch… perhaps she hadn't the energy.

Bath over with no upchuck. Ma had said no milk for her as long as there was fever, and the fever was down below a hundred… almost. How about cheese? She remembered her sister toasting a split biscuit and topping with melted cheese… Maybe…? Even a bite or two would be a plus and maybe make them both feel better.

Quickly cutting the soft interior from a biscuit, she placed it against the iron stove lid, and it was toasted to a golden tan in a minute. She lay rat-trap cheese on top and watched it melt into the pores of the bread. Hmmm, smelled heavenly. Breaking it into tiny crumbs, she took the bowl to the bed.

"I made myself some bread and cheese… want a taste?"

Laverne wasn't sure… but was obviously tempted. She agreed on a bite about the size of Rowenna's thumbnail. A small amount of effort sent it down with a grimace of pain but not a shriek. She opened her mouth for another bite.

Rowenna allowed another few bites and set it aside. They must save room for liquid so Ma would be happy. Another half a cup of the orange seltzer and her patient was drooping wearily as a clipped daisy out of water.

All right, Rowenna, she chided herself. *Don't get too excited feeding her. You'll have it in your lap to clean up and then have to start over.* Quietly she set the liquid aside and snugged the covers up under the red-pimply chin as her patient turned her face to the wall. Rowenna was so excited with the improvement that she wanted to burst out into joyous song but instead opted for a gentle hum.

It was late afternoon, so what she needed at the store before tomorrow, she'd better get right now and let the magazines wait. It was going to be a long evening with lots of time to kill.

Gun in pocket, she raced down to the A&P. Six oranges, six eggs and a can of peaches. Quick stop at the barber's for two of the tiny seltzer bottles. Dash back to the cabin. Patient still asleep.

She whipped a half-batch of cornbread and baked it in the iron skillet. She opened the can of peaches and settled at the table for a leisurely meal with the magazines. She bowed her head over the steaming cornbread… a favorite of hers… and realized that just bowing reverently would not be enough. Heaven deserved more than that.

Stepping out of the cabin, she looked up toward the evening sky at the red clouds spread like ribbons across the lavender horizon.

"Angel, did you see what just happened… with my sister? Did you have anything to do with that? I was so… so… discouraged because I don't know what I'm doing, and I keep thinking I'm going to mess up and make her worse. Is she better, or is it just because I'm hoping so much?"

The chill October breeze filtered through the trees and brought a shiver. "Uh… Angel… when you see your Boss, will you ask if it's all right for me to learn how to take care of sick people…? The right way, I mean. And I need to know quickly, if possible."

The smell of the wood smoke from many chimneys mixed with the chill in the air and somehow brought a sense of peace. The girl felt her face crumble into sobs of relief and the tears streamed down her face. What was going on? Why would she cry when she was so happy? Hurriedly wiping her tears on her sleeve, she turned toward the door.

Could she really ask for something weird like information and expect to get it? She was just a fourteen-year-old girl in a tiny town in a small state in the middle of God's big planet. How could she expect to be heard with all God had to do… but there were the angels. Granddad had told her and Wally when they were little that angels were everywhere. She really hadn't paid much attention at the time. But now, maybe…?

At that time, two hollows over to the east in the town of Wishbone, Wally knelt before the marquee sign sorting out the letters and thinking of his cousin who was so good at it.

He needed the letters for 'STUDY TO SHOW YOURSELF APPROVED.'

Hmmm. Well… study hall inside the church doors now? Letters put in place, he stood back and looked at it, feeling that it might have been selected just for him. But what was it he must study? He was years out of school and hadn't really studied anything since then and hadn't planned to. His life was going in exactly the right direction. If he kept at it, there would likely be a job for him right here in his own town for the rest of his life.

So why was he feeling that the period he had placed after the sentence of his public schooling might need to have been a comma instead? Hmmmm.

STUDY, TO SHOW THYSELF APPROVED. 2 TIMOTHY 2:15

Laverne actually stood up on her bedroom rug without help. Not for long, and actually not so steady, but it was now the end of the second week. It was only occasionally that her temp went over one hundred point five.

She was able to sleep without groaning and demanded to be allowed to take her own daily bath. Her nurse agreed on the condition that she be allow to watch to be sure she used both soaps thoroughly and the healing rinse. Otherwise, she'd strike out over the hills and tell Ma. Laverne actually grinned a bit at that.

A few days ago, Ma had sent Pa over with what may have been a life saver food-wise. He brought a dozen jars of home-canned applesauce from the Ben Davis trees on the hillside. Ma's note said that when Laverne was a toddler, she loved smooth applesauce heated with a lot of butter and a little cinnamon. Ma had said to push the apples through the strainer to be entirely without lumps, and don't let her have more than one cupful at a time.

Rowenna became wide-eyed eager over that. Her patient hadn't eaten over a half a cup of anything since she had come. A whole cup! Really! Thank you, Angel, or whoever reminded Ma of what Rowenna would never have known about. It worked!

After the first two cups, being dinner and supper, Rowenna stirred an egg into the next one before heating it, and Laverne never tasted the difference. It was rather a feeling in her family that if an ill member could manage to eat an egg, it was a sign they would get well.

And she even ate a few bites of mashed potato, heavily buttered. Two days ago she had demanded, and finally received, her hand mirror, and Rowenna would never forget the tortured crumbling of facial features as her sister's agony revealed itself. Purple skin, scabby and rough. Her life's choice of a profession required her to be beautiful, and she was certainly not. If that wasn't enough, her weight loss had turned her features into a whole other person. For the next two days, she wallowed in her misery.

When she had sobbed herself to sleep at last, Rowenna was back on her thinking stool, staring down at her sleeping sister. What could she do to help? *Angel... can you find out for me if she will be beautiful again? Don't bother about improving me, but please, please don't leave her with scars. Can you do that...* Rowenna clenched her teeth with concern. Was she asking too much? She was being terribly bold in calling on the heavenly beings the way she was.

Actually, she really needed a book about the most common illnesses and the best thing to do for them. Of course, Ma, having reared 13 children, knew a lot, but she might forget an important detail... like the applesauce.

She just had to have a book that she could hold in her hand with words that she could read. She understood books. They were friends. She had met a lot of them in the schoolhouse, and books had been her close friends ever since.

Easing quietly down from the stool, she slipped into the kitchen and the lovely pile of magazines with their words and colored pictures. Her school friend, Jewelee, was studying... Wally was working... her sister was sleeping... and she was quarantined in the house by the stinking measles. But she had magazines! No matter that they were ragged, out-of-date and dog-eared!

She pulled her chair up to the table by the west window and turned page after page. Stories that she might... or not... read later. Now she just wanted to relax, think on nothing, and turn the pages.

There was a place where you could order embroider patterns, and some kind of medicine that would cure any disease if it was just taken right. There were things to put in your shoes to make you taller and some scissors so strong they could cut tin cans. Hmmm, who would want to do that?

There was a place over in Memphis, Tennessee that had a school to train girls to be nurses. NURSES? Just look at that! A Nurses School? Who knew! It had an address and everything. Maybe they would tell her something. She'd write a request.

Dear Sir or Madam,

I am a fourteen-year-old girl in Arkansas who needs a book about diseases and what to do for people who have them. I know I cannot come to your school, but maybe you can tell me where there is a school that is closer that could help me get the book.

Thank you so much,

Rowenna Moffat

Wishbone, Arkansas

A little scrumbling around and she found an envelope and addressed it to the school. She would be at home before they answered it—if they actually did answer it.

She put down the letter and, with elbows on table and chin in hand, and looked at the evening sky. The afternoon sun was behind a cloud, but the sky was October blue. Rowenna felt her heart beating in her chest, and she had to keep reminding herself to breathe. Could this be an answer? It would be nice if the angel had a message and would just whisper it in her ear. She had an instant and intense desire to tell Granddad what she was doing. He was always interested in whatever she did… or maybe pretended to be.

He was proud when she rescued the kidnapped woman and baby, but if he had not taught her to shoot… and bought her a gun… she could not have done that. With a sigh, she stared at the blue of the sky just as the cloud moved on and the blazing rays of the sun flared out in one direction. As the cloud moved on, the whole circle of the sun came in sight, blazing like fire in the clear, mountain air.

Rowenna picked up her envelope and held it against her beating heart. "Angel, did you do that?" she said out loud in the still room. "If you did, can you do it again?" And the sound of her voice as she asked for something so brave caused trembles all the way down her back.

The blazing white-gold of the sun streamed through the window and was suddenly dimmed by another of the white-cotton clouds. Again the cloud passed by and released the blazing rays onto the earth. Rowenna caught her breath in a sudden gasp... then remembered it was just the clouds blowing across the sky. Only the clouds... NO... it was her answer. Somehow, she was going to get her book.

But was Laverne going to be beautiful again? Was that a selfish thing to ask for? Was there a commandment in the Bible that said not to ask for selfish things for a sister? If she could only ask Granddad... he would understand why she needed to know.

Wally Hopkins finished the marquee sign and stood looking at it. It was only a sign, the kind Preacher Harvey Clemmons liked. He wanted the town's folks to think about his signs longer than a glance.

Wally thought. If he needed to study, what would he be studying about? He had hardly been big enough to remember Granddad's sermons, though most folks thought he was a good preacher... just got too old and tired. Wally did well in school... well, maybe not the top, but he held his own. So what was left that he needed to learn?

He was sure Preacher Harvey was referring to the Bible, and that was one book that Wally had trouble getting interested in. Either things had already happened, and they were mildly interesting... or were going to happen, and who knew when? Wally was highly interested in what was happening right now, and he loved it. The WM was just about the best place in town to work. He was grateful for the privilege and occasionally remembered to be thankful.

Jadeen felt that now, after two and a half weeks, it was time to remind the town of Wishbone that the measles epidemic was still far away, thanks to her sister, the Girl with the Gun. Perhaps another word or two just to make certain she would not be shunned because of something that might be 'catching'.

CLASSIFIED ADVERTISMENTS

Ripe thin-shelled pecans. You pick 'em before the squirrels and the crows. Fifty cents a bushel. Bascoms on Winding Lane. Come any day this week.

Paint pony ready to be broke. Swap for butcher goats or what-have-you. I'll have the pony down by the Big Three on Thursday. Jack Massengar.

Need a couch that makes a bed. Leave message with Thimbles and Spools.

Church sign: "A bit of kneeling will keep you in good standing. Come here next Sunday for proof."

PUBLIC NOTICE: Wishbone is still safe from the measles, and the Girl with the Gun is still on the job. She has another ten days to go. We wish her well and are proud of her success.

Stove wood by the rick. Your land or mine. Oak, elm or pecan. Two dollars a rick, delivered. Riley Brothers. Leave your order with Carpenter Shop.

And others….

In this way, the town of Wishbone was permitted to breathe a sigh of relief that they had been protected from this measles outbreak. One could almost picture the Girl with the Gun aiming at those old germs and shooting them down before they could attack anyone.

On the eighteenth day of her quarantine, Laverne was faithfully doing the soaping and rinsing. Rowenna tried to quietly observe, and it seemed that the purple skin had more of a yellow cast in the dim light. Bruised skin often turned yellow as it began to heal, especially on light-complexioned people. She said nothing, though, for fear of setting off another bout of depression.

There was always another meal facing them. How did her ma ever survive all of those years with the cooking she had to do?

Let's see, Laverne was getting a lot better. Maybe, well, "Say, what if I skipped down to the A&P and got a chicken? We could have dumplings for supper. What do you think?" She directed the question to her patient.

Her patient looked interested. She was getting a bit weary of rice and potatoes, juice and eggs.

"We could have egg salad for lunch if you think you can eat mustard, and the chicken would be ready by evening. Actually, I make fairly good dumplings."

She grabbed up her letter as she left the cabin. She would mail it on the way to the A&P. "What do you think, Angel? Could I have an answer by the time Pa comes after me?"

She really didn't expect another flash of sunshine as a heavenly answer. She was just being conversational with the angel. She also didn't expect to be greeted by the seven different people who recognized her as the Girl with the Gun. That Jadeen! At it again!

The early dark was setting in as Rowenna dished up two bowls of the rich broth, dumplings and pieces of fall-from-the-bone, tender chicken. Choosing her sister's largest plates as trays, she carried them to the bedroom.

Laverne was in such a good humor that Rowenna ate as slowly as possible to prolong the meal. Surprisingly, they found things to talk about without mentioning measles even one time.

THE HILLTOP HOUSE IN WISHBONE

It was no real surprise when the package came to the Moffat house on the hill. The home address was occasionally used by any of the thirteen children, but for a small package to come for Rowenna, when she was not even at home, spawned a bit of thought.

What had she ordered and why... and should it be taken to her? But it didn't look urgent, and she would be home in a week, bringing Laverne if she wanted to come.

And it appeared to be from... hmmm... a nursing school...? In Memphis, Tennessee...? What are they doing writing to our barely fourteen-year-old girl?

If the return address of the school had not been plainly on the package, they would have immediately opened it... for after all, they were parents, and parents were responsible for under-aged children. But, with a tense sigh, they set it aside to wait for her.

Meanwhile, three hollows to the west, the morning bath continued with the younger sister still monitoring every movement. It really looked like the spots were fading, but she was afraid to get her sister's hopes up. But just look, the spaces between the bumps were almost the normal color of her skin, and she hadn't had a fever in four days. Not even a little one.

It seemed Ma's remote control of the disease was right-on perfect, and the overworked doctor in Eureka had not even been consulted. See there? Some things can be taken care of without a doctor, if one just knows what to do, or has someone like Ma to tell them. That's all it took to be a nurse.

And the end of this confinement was staring her in the face… or maybe the thoughts. Home. Would there be something from the nursing school… or not…? Probably not. What right had she to expect such special attention?

So what was next? She had searched the ragged magazines, but there was not one other shred of useful information. So what now? "The eye of the Lord…."

Why do I keep thinking of that verse? I have always known about the Lord's eyes. They told me that as a little girl.

But then the voice in her head argued… *"But you're a big girl now. So think about something beside the compound eyes of a fly. The fly is tiny and needs those eyes to escape the swatter. How about the eye of an eagle…? It flies high and searches the earth for food for the hatchlings in the nest. Does that give you any ideas?"*

Hmmmm, do you mean that I am a hatchling still in the nest?

"…what do you think? Do you feel like a hatchling…?"

Uh… well, sort of.

"…and eventually the hatchling grows strong enough to fly. Then it can find its own food."

Rowenna shuddered and shook her head. What was the voice trying to say to her? Of course the 'food' could not be biscuits and gravy… or mashed potatoes. It had to mean… what? Information? *Well, just think of the times I've run to Granddad with questions. And tomorrow Pa comes to get me, and the next day I'll see Granddad. He'll expect it.*

Then came the wide-open-eyed startle. *Will there be a time when Granddad can't help me?* Horrifying thought, and she patted the comforting lump in her pocket for which she thanked him. At this point, she seemed almost undressed without it.

The voice again. "…*when the hatchlings grow feathers and strong wings, they no longer need help that they cannot get for themselves.…*"

Now, that was too hard to consider, so she tossed her head, moving the voice away so she could gather her things and give the cabin one last cleaning. She was somewhat surprised that Laverne had consented to go to the hilltop house for a week. This illness had apparently shaken her to her bones… and her being such a confident and headstrong girl. Another week, with Ma around, would set her up to meet the world again.

And Laverne looked forward. By then the theaters would start up again with new vigor. There were even 'summer people' in the winter, especially Christmas week. But she was forced to smile at how her relationship with her sister had been. Actually, Rowenna was a rather clever and interesting person, and Laverne sincerely did not want her to also be interested in the theater. She had a way about her… and it was a way that Laverne did not wish to compete with.

But farthest from her sister's mind was acting. The plays were fun to watch, but then one must go home and get on with life. And say, when she got home, she could help Wally with his church marquees again! Life back to normal.

And that very day, Wally was looking forward to her return as he sorted through the box of letters for the right ones. Preacher Clemmons had interesting statements sometimes. This one was sure to catch a few of the town's people off guard.

Wally sorted out the 's' letters to be ready. "Christ's return is near. Don't miss it for the world!" And he got to use the only exclamation point in the set. The good old 'ball and bat' to sock folks' attention right between the eyes!

But every time he knelt on the grass to change the letters, he was again stuck with the impact of "Study to show yourself approved." It was exasperating. 'Study' what? And who was going to approve or disapprove? Wally really hated thoughts like that.

He liked the solid feel of the cans and the shelves… of the bookkeeping and the money… and even the sure steps of the mare called Mountain Minnie. She hadn't started out with that name, but her name (Minerva) was changed by Nathan when he noted that she was the most sure-footed transportation for the mountains that the WM had.

But now, Wally had the mountain trips to make, and he appreciated the sure-footed animal. In fact, when he finished with the letters, he would be getting things together to leave at first light in the morning to go after the eggs. Why did the best chicken farmer have to live on the tip-top peak of Temple Hill, the one that was made of rocks?

But he knew why... nothing else would grow up there, but the hens thrived and produced the large, brown eggs that the Wishbone cooks preferred. Also, they had that wonderful rock-enclosed cave that kept the eggs cool in the summer and from freezing in the winter.

Maybe while climbing up the stony ledges he would finally be able to get rid of that pesky thought that was digging its own furrow through his mind.

Pa Moffat cheerfully collected his daughters and sighed with relief when he saw Laverne. Only a few faintly off-colored spots on her neck and arms. Her face was as clear and beautiful as ever... not that he cared, but he knew of its importance to her.

By late afternoon, he deposited the pair at the porch of the hilltop house and trotted the buggy on back to the shed. Peppersauce was still bouncy and eager. She was certainly one fine little pony, and he selected one of the late Ben Davis apples for her... that he kept at the barn for such a purpose.

She crunched the crisp fruit, foamy juice dripping as she looked at Pa with her wonderful eyes. Pa patted her face... and then her rounded rump... and headed for the house.

Rowenna was just opening the puzzling package. Her glance told her that it would not be all bad... at least they had answered. Maybe it held a catalog of what she could order, but no... out slid the slick-covered book with pictures of medicine bottles on the front and back.

Forcing herself to leave the book unopened, she read the letter.

DEAR MISS MOFFAT:

We were extremely pleased to receive your query but regret to tell you that we are not in the business of selling books.

We are a school for resident students, and we joyfully look forward to having you here in a few years. We admit anyone who has completed their eight years of education and is between the ages of eighteen and twenty one.

However, as a token of our appreciation for your interest, we are enclosing our Manual of Common Diseases and their Best Treatment. Also included in this book is first aid advice for injuries and childbirth without the assistance of a midwife. It is the chapter "What to Do Until the Midwife Comes."

We hope this book will partly make up for the disappointing information we are forced to send you, but hope to see you when you can manage it.

Memphis School of Nursing

Memphis, Tennessee

Three pairs of eyes watched as Rowenna silently read the bad news. Pa, Ma and Laverne stared as her face registered the sadness she felt, then she handed the letter to Pa, who read it aloud.

While he read, Rowenna thumbed through the pages of the new book. Just look at that! Measles, whooping cough, chicken pox... all were there and a description of each followed. Suggestions for care of the ill. The necessity of cleanliness. How many of the diseases were transmitted.

A long, deep sigh. It was rather like the first bite of a perfectly browned biscuit spread with liberal amounts of butter. The book was extremely satisfying and a thoughtful gift from the school, but it only made her want more.

It might be like the aroma of sausage on a cold winter morning when one has been doing barn chores. While stomping the dirt from your boots in the mud room, you knew from the aroma of the sausage that there would be eggs and biscuits and likely a mound of cottage-fried potatoes.

And now... even more, she must go see Granddad. Show him the book... ask him a few important questions. And into her head popped the pesky voice: *"…just like the hatchlings in the nest, eyes searching the skies, knowing where their food comes from…"* She knew. That would be Granddad.

Now Ma was examining the book, turning the pages slowly and nodding approval. Laverne made her way to the kitchen, snooping in kettles and obeying the demands of her returning appetite. A good sign… If there was anything Ma knew about… it was food.

Rowenna unpacked her boxes and sorted her underwear to be sudsed out and hung on the line before she headed down the hill. Her whole body longed for the walk down the familiar path to the town, almost a half a mile away. The month of being cooped up like a broody hen waiting for eggs to hatch was about all a wandering country girl could stand. Maybe she'd borrow Mustard and climb the chinky pin hill, but first must be the 'thank you' letter.

Dear Sir or Madam:

I do sincerely thank you for the wonderful gift of the book of Common Diseases. It will go far toward answering a lot of questions in my mind.

Now, if I may be so very bold, I would like to ask you one more question. Is it against your rules to send me the name and address of the publisher where you buy your books? I would so much love to have them that I will attempt to order them for myself if I may learn the address of that company.

I thank you so much for your time and once more for the wonderful gift of the book. I may never get to attend your school, but I will never forget the kind people who decided to help me in this way.

Most Sincerely,

Rowenna Moffat

Wishbone, Arkansas

Now on to town to mail the letter and check in with Granddad. There was a wonderful thing about granddads... they mostly had time for you. Pa's were good but much too busy for the thirteenth kid. Especially as she got older and her questions grew harder.

First question for him would be... "Would it be all right to ask to find out if I'm thinking in the right direction? Maybe I should just be thankful for my book and let it go."

The old man wisely answered her question with a question: "Will it be possible, truly, for you to forget something so important to you? Think about it before you answer."

She did. "But, Granddad, I actually thought of Gideon and the fleece*, but I knew I was not important enough to bother God with my own questions."

Granddad nodded. "I can fully understand that, being that you are not as important as a sparrow**, and God said he saw each one as it finally fell to the earth."

A sigh and a frown of exasperation. "But Granddad, I can't really ask God for something so simple as a way to get the books I want."

And, again, Granddad nodded agreeably. "Perhaps not, if that's the way you feel. It might depend on how important it is to you. I can't answer for God, but I can't see why it would a problem for God to let you to know if you were starting down the wrong path or the right one."

"You mean I can ask my angel to see if I can get what I want?"

"My dear, it's all right to ask, but you must be prepared to wait for the answer and also be prepared for it when it comes. It might not be the way you hope it will be. Why don't you take Mustard and go for a climb? He hasn't been out for more than a month, and he's getting fat and lazy."

Mustard might have been the happiest creature in the town to see her. With much head-tossing and rippling of lips, and with a fair amount of pleased grumbling deep in his throat, he tried to assist her with the bridle and saddle and joyfully headed for the hills.

It was mid-November, and the trees were either brilliant with fall colors or bare of limbs where the leaves had blown away. The purple asters were still holding their blooms and tempting the miniature, butter-yellow butterflies and awaiting the final visits from the bees.

Young rabbits were striving to put on fat for the leanness of the winter. A few of them would likely be with her as she would later climb the path to hilltop house and home. Mustard could spend the night with Peppersauce and old Poppyseed, the roan mare with the wealth of black freckles on legs and face. Hard to believe that Poppyseed was Peppersauce's mother.

With a few random thoughts of 'how does one know if they are important enough to be heard,' she rode along. Was that just a concern of a thirteenth kid… or one trying to understand a relationship with a heavenly being? But, after a while, she settled down to enjoying the familiar sights of Wishbone and realizing how fortunate she was to have been born in a tiny Arkansas town.

She'd visit the Thimbles and Spools on the way home. The aunts loved her visits and so quickly took her problems as their problems… but she would not concern them with her current problem. They would just be distressed that they had no answer for her. What did they know of angels…?

And it was now, on this deliciously mild day in mid-November, that cousin Wally boarded Mountain Minnie after affixing the pack for the egg crates. Each crate held 144 eggs… one gross, as he remembered from school. The two crates furnished the WM with a week's supply of eggs… if the weather permitted the trip to the mountain.

Occasionally, in the winter, he would make two trips in one week just in the event of a freeze-up that coated the stony ledges with a sheet of frozen crystal. It was really a neat pack that had been invented by Nathan when he was making the trips. Padded for the comfort of the animal and solidly braced for the protection of the fragile egg shells, it rode safely on Mountain Minnie's ample rear.

This was a lovely day, and the purple asters popped out from every rock crevasse and covered themselves with the starry blossoms. Wally gave a half a minute of thought as to how the tiny yellow fall butterflies knew just when to come for the last taste of nectar before winter killed them.

Nearing the top of Temple Hill, the butterflies were joined by the bees belonging to the egg farmer. This farmer was the only customer who insisted on feeding him when he came... and when was an a sixteen-year-old boy not hungry? What would it be served today? Their breaded pork chops were the stuff of dreams, but their pepper-meatloaf was not far behind.

And two hours later, stomach comfortably stretched, he headed for the valley and the WM. Strangely, the downhill trip was always slower than the climb, as Mountain Minnie was strategically careful with her hoof placement. Her broad, comfortable body moved with graceful strength, making her a dream to ride, and Wally should know. He'd had been riding horses for the last ten years.

The view from the mountain was spectacular in the late fall when all leaves but the black oak had fallen. He could see three mountaintops to the east, each outlined with a softer shade of blue. Wishbone's two rivers were sparkling ribbons below, and the buildings of the town like a child's toys.

Mountain Minnie had no need of human guidance, as she had made this trip more than a hundred times, and there was absolutely no place to go except the path that had been chipped out of the mountain stones by long-ago inhabitants.

She allowed Wally the opportunity to study the unique scenery. Study? There it was again, and he was getting purely tired of the subject. He frowned and demanded of the air around him, "Either let me know what's going on or leave me alone!"

Mountain Minnie flicked her ears at his voice, but none of the words meant anything to her, so she plodded onward, testing the footing with each hoof placement. She stepped down from a 6-inch ledge and settled herself firmly on the next flat stone sheet.

What happened next was as much a surprise to her as it was to Wally as he suddenly left the saddle behind... landing on his rear on a loose pile of shale and scooted downward. The next action was not a surprise, as every mountain lad knows that loose shale gravel, being smooth and slick, can only go downward, sliding on their own slickly-shining surfaces. This shale was no exception.

On his backside and elbows, he moved downward, searching with feet and hands for something to stop the slide... and reaching nothing. One knee collided with a solid boulder and tipped him to his left shoulder. A thorn caught on his shirt sleeve, making a three-cornered snag before letting loose. A dip in the landscape turned him face down, scooting on his elbows and ineffectively digging toes into the rocks searching for any kind of crevasse.

Eventually there should be a tree... and there was. With a final scrape and jerk away from a second thorn bush, he landed on his rear again, his back firmly against the trunk of a sassafras tree. He could smell the fragrance of sassafras tea from the fallen leaves he had slid through.

First in his concern was the condition of the 288 large brown eggs, and he cast an apprehensive glance upward. From about sixty feet above, Mountain Minnie stood looking down at him with puzzled eyes. Humans were so strange and did such unexpected things sometimes. So now... did he want her to come down there?

Looking this way and that for a safe foothold, Wally saw her intention. He could only shout, "NO! STAY! Whoa. Minnie, whoa... whoa! WAIT! GOOD GIRL! WHOA!"

The ever-obedient mare paused, one experimental hoof raised, and attempted to determine what this human wanted. She knew *Whoa*, and *Good Girl*, and it was a rough path down to him, so she thought she'd just wait for further clarification.

Wally righted his battered body, bleeding elbow and torn shirt... rear pocket hanging by a thread... and turned his face toward climbing upward. His boot toes searching for footholds and his hands grasping sprouts and weeds, he inched his way, shouting comforting encouragement to the mare.

Her long brown face with dark, liquid eyes continued to follow his progress, her lips rippling with sounds of sympathy. Really, he needn't have done that... she would willingly take him anywhere. So she continued to stare, her equine brain mentally assisting him along the way. He seemed to be making progress.

Finally, as he reached for the ledge at Mountain Minnie's hooves, he asked himself, "WHAT is going on?" He had never before slipped (been thrown?) from the saddle like that, and certainly not from a patient, sure-footed mare as she picked her safe way down the mountain. For strange happenings along the way, he rather well mimicked Saul of Tarsus on his way to persecute the Christians.***

So strange to think of that interesting story from his childhood… how Saul was causing all kinds of trouble, thinking he was doing God a favor. And how God had to cause blindness to get his attention. When he couldn't see anything else, then God could tell him what he wanted him to do.

Mountain Minnie snorted conversationally as her rider pulled himself to a standing position… pant knees caked with dirt, elbow bleeding and chin skinned. A pump-knot was forming on the back of his head from the tree trunk, and his hair littered with sticks and broken leaves. Hat! Where was it? And a glance downward revealed only the scuffed-up path his body had taken. Oh, well.

Turning to the patient horse, he saw… there, pegged on the saddle horn, was his hat. Totally undamaged. Irritatedly, he jammed the hat on his head and leaped into the saddle between the two gross of brown eggs.

Mountain Minnie turned her head to him with a tolerant expression that could have been asking, "Now… have we gotten that over with so we can go on down the hill?"

"Come on, Minnie. Let's go." She turned her long, brown face forward but was not yet comfortable. She turned again to him, slowly blinking her dark eyes. Finally satisfied that things were back on track, she turned forward and placed her worn hooves onto the safe parts of the trail that she knew so well.

Wally, trying to be grateful that the expensive 288 eggs were still safely within their brown shells, returned his attention to his strange escapade. Was that any more strange than cousin Row thinking she was being nudged by an angel? With questions she knew not…? Not really… because Row knew what she wanted, and she was just stubborn enough and patient enough to manage to get it.

While he, on the other hand, already had exactly what he wanted, and he had tried to remember to be properly grateful. There wasn't anything to 'study' to do a better job than he was doing, and he was very ready to advance as soon as a vacancy occurred by Nathan managing to get what he wanted.

Still puzzling over circumstances, Wally arrived at the WM and carefully off-loaded his cargo. Nathan took one look at him and demanded, "What happened to you? Did you meet a bear... or a panther?"

Wally was in no mood to explain. "Little problem with a bush."

Nathan knew there was much more to know, but he could wait. As near as he could remember, there were no thorn bushes on that mountain path up Temple Hill.

And Jadeen did her part.

CLASSIFIED ADVERTISEMENTS

Stove wood delivered. Hardwood or soft. Leave message at the Carpenter Shop.

Fresh shipment of oranges, grapefruit and lemons at the WM. Also shredded coconut and brown sugar. Free with each purchase, the recipe for Candied Citrus Peels. Ask for it.

Newsbreak: The Girl with the Gun and her beautiful actress-sister are at home for a few days. Look quick if you want to see either of them, as they can disappear in a minute.

Walnuts, hickory nuts and chinky pins, cleaned and hulled, ready for Christmas baking. Also sassafras tea harvested at its best and sealed in jars for the flavor. Good for gifts or just for enjoying. Also peanut brittle by the pound.

Church marquee: "Do you spell your best friend 'DOG' or 'GOD'?"

Thick, warm knitted caps for children; also winter gowns for babies. Good gifts for new mothers. Other surprises at Thimbles and Spools.

And more....

There were those who waved to Rowenna and commented that she might not be home long... as least, that's what the Cryer had said. What could the girl do but shrug and smile? Jadeen did not act with malice but only needed something to say in the Classifieds so the world would remember where and who she was. So interesting to Rowenna that her sisters both loved attention while she roamed the woodlands alone, struggling with her own thoughts.

It was barely past the first week of December that the next thing happened. Rowenna had spent the day with the aunts. They were in their elements of joy when the girl agreed that the new gun holster would answer a problem that had hung in the minds of the aunts.

They had created a gun-shaped pocket that attached to an under-dress belt. If Rowenna's skirt had any fullness at all, it successfully hid any trace of the weapon and still was within handy reach if needed.

Of course, it meant that if she suddenly needed the weapon, she must lift her skirt to reach the handle, but none of this mattered if she wore a pettislip that maintained her modesty. And if she had no suitable pettislips, dear, they would provide them forthwith, and we'll just take the measurements now to be ready.

The girl had left the aunts and helped Wally with the church marquee. She could see he was not particularly happy with what they wrote, but she had her own problems. In fact, she fully agreed with every word of the selection.

It had so many letters; she had done a lot of sorting and had to dip into the back-stock, and Wally had to scrunch the words close to get it all on there.

"God doesn't always call the qualified, but he always qualifies the called."

Wally knew God was trying to tell him something, and he was trying not to listen... all the time being concerned that God's next attempt to get his attention might be worse than the spill up on Temple Hill. Blind... maybe? Like Saul/Paul? Or a broken leg? Maybe being fired from his job?

All that while Rowenna climbed to the hilltop house deep in thought. What was next? Granddad seemed to think she should feel free to do as Gideon did to learn an answer, if she just didn't demand that God do what she wanted. And what did she want? A place to buy the books and enough money to do it.

Granddad seemed to think it was alright but insisted that the decision must be hers. He suggested that what she asked was a 'tall order' for a fourteen-year-old, and maybe she was meant to wait until she was eighteen.

So, mind whirling with thought, she climbed the hill. Now in sight of the big house and its surrounding buildings, she saw a strange horse. A beautiful chestnut stallion with a new saddle and a lot of silver on the bridle. A horse to be proud of, and her owner was truly that.

A man she did not know stood on the porch talking with Pa, seemingly ready to leave but, seeing her, changed his mind.

Pa called her to come on in to the parlor. Hmmm, well….

The man looked at her and began, "Miss Rowenna, I find myself in need of your help if you can see your way clear. The Cryer said you wasn't to be around long, so I hurried right over. Like I was sayin' to your pa, you'd be the one we need after readin' how you took care'a your sister with the hard red measles. We ain't for sure yet, but we may have a case of them measles… anyway, we got a sick girl."

Pa butted in to help. "This here's Abe Parnell from over to Dead Horse Springss. Now I said to 'im the decision'd be yours, and you might not want to be away from home for Christmas, with the other's comin' home and all. Now, he'll tell you what he needs."

She turned back the fidgety man who stood on one foot, then the other. "It's my little girl who took on a fever. My wife could'a managed but for the little fellow that's three and the old billy goat that forced her into a bind and broke her foot. Mostly she needs help with the girl, and you, takin' care of that kidnapped woman and then your sister… you'd be the first in our mind to have if you could be spared for … well, for a while, anyway."

"Measles? You think…."

He nodded sadly. "We let her visit her cousin in Eureka. Got'er back quick as we heard. She should'a come down with 'em sooner, and that made us wonder what it was. The little fellow, he's a live wire, and we been tyin' 'im up, his ma not bein' able to chase 'im. We're needin' help in the worst way."

He waited a quiet minute. "So if you're knowin' it's not somethin' you can do, I'll need to be lookin' and don't know which way to go. If you could see your way clear, we'd be payin' you, of course, and you'd have the private room we made for her old ma, who's gone on to her reward."

Ma was looking from Rowenna to the man and then to Pa, concern written all over her face. "You fellows knowin' she's only fourteen? That's a lot for a girl no older's that."

Mr. Parnell turned a sad face toward Ma. "But, Miz Moffat, that girl's a month older'n she was when you trusted her with her sister, and you not even in the same town. I can promise I'll be there every night. I'd stop what I do and stay with them myself, but I'm a woodcutter and I have orders for wood stacked up to be doin'. If I stayed home, I'd not have the money and the customers'd not have the wood." He paused, staring out over the valley with worried eye, then continued....

"Time I was a little sprout, my pa'd take us over to hear Preacher Hopkins times he could get through the valley. I always looked forward to that like a treat."

Pa brightened. "You knew Preacher Hopkins? And you'd be home every night, and she'd have a private room to sleep in?"

The man nodded, eagerly.

Pa looked at Rowenna. "You've got to decide, Reena. I can't tell you what to do when you're needed. This here's a neighbor, and I'm thinkin' you're the best he could find. Leastwise, that's what I thought when we sent you to Eureka, and that turned out well. You seem to be old enough for the job, so you decide."

Rowenna looked at her ma. The familiar face took on a small smile and her head a faint nod. She was agreeing with Pa, though she was wishing she didn't have to.

Rowenna, her heart pounding in her chest, turned to the man. "Mr. Parnell, if you think I can be a help, I'll come and do what I can." The back of her mind wished for Granddad and an answer from him, but the voice had told her that eventually the baby eagles had to find their own food. Now, what did that have to do with what she had just agreed to?

The man looked at Rowenna with pathetic gratefulness in his eyes. "Guess it'd be right to say one more thing so your folks could hear. My wife, she's… well, it's just that… I should tell you she's in a family way, but not due for a whole month."

Rowenna glanced back toward her ma and saw the shiver pass from her head to her feet, but she said nothing. Ma was having a terrible time agreeing with Pa, but she was doing her best.

Rowenna looked back toward the man. "I'll come and do my best. I'd better go pack, and I guess Pa knows where you live." She turned and left, the very floor feeling strange under her feet. Strangers. A family with sickness. A toddler, and she had no experience there. A woman on crutches. WHAT IN THE WORLD was she DOING?

First into the box was Florence Nightingale, Clara Barton and the book on common diseases. Next was ammo for her 22mm Winchester. On top of that came her clothes. And she was ready.

It was a silent father and daughter trip up to Dead Horse Springss. The little farm site was just about as far from anything at all as one could get. The thing was, though, it was totally surrounded with trees, and that's what furnished the family livelihood.

As they entered the yard of the Parnell house… with Mr. Parnell waiting to greet them, Pa reached across the buggy seat with his large, work-calloused hand and enclosed one of hers. Leaning toward her, he whispered, "I'm very proud of you."

Rowenna felt the tears fill her eyes, but she refused to let them fall. She wanted nothing more than to throw herself at her father's chest and weep away the next month.

Instead, she lifted her head, firmed her lips and smiled.

*Judges, chapter 6: specifically verses 37-40
**Matthew, chapter 10: specifically verses 29-31
***Acts, chapter 9: specifically verses 3-6

DEAD HORSE SPRINGS

It was not a town… mainly just a designated place among the hills and hollows of convoluted soil and flint rock of northwestern Arkansas. Dead Horse Springss was a mountain saddle composed of farms, each with 40 to 50 acres each. This consequently separated the dwellings to the extent of having no neighbors closer than about three miles.

The Parnell place was a log cabin with extended ells and an elevated room with windows facing out over the wide valley. Pa, having received orders not to be around the afflicted child, hugged her goodbye in the yard, turned and wiped his sleeve across his eyes and stepped into the buggy. Peppersauce was ready and tripped lightly up to the Ridge that would take her home.

Mrs. Parnell ("call me Emily") stood on the wide porch leaning heavily on her crutch. Her left foot was bound tightly in elastic binding, and her dress had been let out to the furtherest extent of its size. A small boy clung to the back of her skirt.

"So wonderful to have you, my dear," were Emily's first words as she reached for Rowenna's hand and lifted it to her cheek with a grateful expression. "Abe'll bring your things in, and we'll get you set up in the upper room. It's a nice room, and I hope you'll like it. We built it up there so my old ma could spend her last days with us. It's warmer than the other rooms."

It was evident that Emily was having an attack of nerves and was speaking just to have a sound in the air. By comparison, it was likely she was even more nervous than Rowenna.

"I'm sure it'll be fine. I'm just here to tend the little girl, if I can. Can I see her first off?"

"Yes, certainly. I should have offered. Come right in here."

Down a short hall was a small room, obviously meant for a little girl. On the bed she lay, her face a flaming red. Rowenna lifted her arm, fully expecting to see the purple bumps under her arm, and was not mistaken. She had already recognized the familiar smell. This would clearly not do. How could she tend the girl way back here and sleep upstairs... but did she have the right to demand she be moved? Wait....

Squaring her shoulders and pulling her wits together, she told herself, *I am hired to do what I can do, so that gives me the right.*

"Uh... ma'am... Emily. I have to say this. You must let me have the little girl in the same room as I am, or I cannot take care of her." She waited for the verdict.

Emily glanced around in the tiny room. "But there ain't no room for another bed. Maybe we could…."

"Could she be moved upstairs with me? That looks like a much bigger room."

Emily looked dismayed. "But… you see, I can't be goin' up the stairs like I am. So I…."

Be brave, Rowenna. Say it. "Mrs. Parnell, are you afraid for me to take care of your little girl by myself? I can understand it if you feel that way, and Mr. Parnell can take me back home and then we…."

"Oh, no! No, please! You must stay. The Cryer said you know what to do [actually it didn't], and I must have help. Quick as she ran a fever, we got scared and remembered about you. If she's upstairs, I can't even help you if you needed it. That was sort of what I thought…."

Rowenna knew it wasn't, but it was a good escape. "I'll make a deal with you. If we need help, it will likely be at night, and Mr. Parnell will be here. Would that work?" She was really going out on a limb. Trouble did not happen only at night, but somehow, they must establish an understanding. Quickly.

Emily sniffed and nodded. She'd come up the stairs and help get ready.

Rowenna surprised herself. "No. I can handle it. It will do you no good to be climbin', and if you fell, then think how bad it'd be! I'll go up and look around, and maybe Mr. Parnell could carry the little girl up. My sister couldn't walk for several days without pitching forward on her head. I stayed right with her and gave her baths and treated the itch. I'm sure your little girl will be fine; we just have to just take care of her and wait. What is her name?"

"She's Nancy. I'll go tell Mr. Parnell to take your things upstairs." And she hobbled out of the room on her crutch.

Rowenna sat on the narrow bed beside the little girl. "Nancy? Nancy, honey, my name is Rowenna, and I'm here to help your mama."

The girl peered up at her with red, uninterested eyes. Then closed them and snuggled down in her covers. Fever. Easy to see. She'd see how bad it was just as soon as they got her upstairs where she could get her thermometer. A bath was going to be the first thing after that.

"Honey, we're going to move you upstairs so there'll be more room, and then there'll be a bath for you to make you feel better."

A small ray of interest. "Up to Granny's room? It has good windows."

Huh-oh. Windows. Have to have shades pulled and there likely will not be any. Why would one need shades up here? Newspapers? Towels? Maybe feed sacks from cow feed? Have to make it dark to protect her eyes.

Her pa came to carry her, and he seemed to have no recrimination toward moving her upstairs. Apparently he had convinced himself she was the best they could get… so let her do it. Good.

The upstairs room was lovely. Nice curtains. Shame to cover them, but it had to be. "Mr. Parnell, these windows will have to be darkened while she's broken out. Sometimes measles makes weak eyes, the books say." At least her ma and the new book agreed on that. The man nodded understanding and left to take care of it.

She had brought the correct soap with her, just in case the Parnells did not have the right kinds. They didn't. Food and liquid. That would be next.

She tucked the little girl into the bed. She seemed even more limp than Laverne had. Truly, the room was quite warm, and what she needed now was warm water.

"Mrs. …I mean, Emily, is she eating anything?"

Emily shook her head sadly.

"Do you have grape juice or blackberry juice…? We'll try a little of that later. Do you have applesauce? Could you push it through a strainer so it is smooth as pudding, and make me a half a cup of warm sauce? I'll put in the butter when I come down to get it. Right now, she's getting a bath."

"A… bath…? With her chillin' and feverin'…?"

Rowenna bravely faced the fearful mother. "Yes, ma'am. I'm afraid so. It's absolutely necessary if I'm to take care of her. If she isn't kept clean, the bumps can re-infect themselves." (Another word from her new book.)

Emily nodded her weary, concerned head. She'd have Abe go to the cave for the apples and fruit juice. She seemed more relaxed now. Small Nancy was not.

When Rowenna approached with the wash pan, the little girl screamed, "No! Go away! I hate you! I want my mama!" Her voice was getting hoarse and was certain to be getting sore. Even the fever can cause sore throat… she had just learned.

Mr. Parnell's face appeared halfway up the stairs. "Everything all right?" he asked conversationally.

"Just fine, thank you. She's going to feel a lot better in about an hour. Then, if the applesauce is ready, we'll try it. And, oh yes, I'm sure you have willow bark for tea. We might need it." Rowenna was amazed at her bravery… to give commands this way. But, of course, it was either that or they could take her home.

Nancy did a fair amount of screaming as she was bathed, but there was no interference from below. Mr. Parnell must have been able to calm Mrs. Parnell. Rowenna came down with the wash water and took back willow bark tea and the applesauce, well buttered.

Rowenna lifted the girl and propped her, half-sitting. It was a lot easier than with Laverne. And they'd need a chamber pot. She'd get it on the next trip down. Hopefully the little girl would be relaxed and sleepy, so her nurse could have supper. An aroma of meatloaf was penetrating the stairway.

Nancy allowed herself to be fed the willow bark tea. Apparently, that was still a well-used item in this household. Aspirin was gaining popularity, but there were some who didn't trust it. It seemed like it might be magic.

A half a cup of tea. Enough. Now a half a cup of apples if she would eat them. No more than that. Rowenna certainly didn't need an upchuck to mess with.

Temperature up. 103 degrees. The book said small children could often produce a temp faster than an adult. Good to know. She went back for cool water and another cloth. Might need it later.

Only two bites of applesauce, but she seemed to like it… just too tired to swallow. Mustn't push her to eat more.

She'd taken aside a half cup of mashed potato to try in the morning. No, Emily, no gravy for her. She might like it, but it has milk. She can't have milk with a fever.

"Oh!" and there was fear in her eyes.

"What's wrong?"

"Just before you got here, I made her drink a cup of milk. I didn't know. I'm so sorry. She likes milk, and I didn't know."

"I know. It's a lot of remember. We'll work on it. A little temp is normal right now. It's the body starting to work. [Oh, the wonderful book!] But we really have to give her liquids."

The upstairs room proved to be a good thing. Emily would not let little Abe Junior climb the stairs. That made it quieter for Nancy. Bumps were rising on the small neck and down her arms. There were a couple of them popping up on her left cheek. She should break out good tomorrow.

Darkness settled onto the hillside farm, and Rowenna lit the candle. There were seven more candles in the bedside stand, so Rowenna felt free to have the light burning to look at her new book. Just for a while. Hardly enough light to read the print, but she could see the boldface headings. Oh, this was going to be so wonderful!

If she was to get only one book, this would be the one she would choose. Tomorrow she might have time to read parts of it. She grinned at the chapter on WHAT TO DO TIL THE MIDWIFE COMES. That should be interesting... as soon as she re-read the chapter on measles.

She blew out the light, finally, and the mountain was quiet except for the night birds. Whip-Will's-Widow out by the barn. A screech owl on down toward the valley. She felt peaceful and fulfilled as she lay beside the sick child. At one point the little girl had snuggled her back against Rowenna. Maybe chills. It seemed that chills and fever were friends, teaming up to cause trouble.

"The eye of the Lord is in every place," even at Dead Horse Springss. It was so strange. She had always known the Lord saw everything, but she didn't really KNOW it as pertained to herself. *If you know where I am, Angel, then you know God intended for me to be here, and you know what I want. I'm not going to bother you anymore about what I want. When it's time, I'll get it.* Rowenna had never even noticed when her urgent desire turned into faith.

It was midnight when Nancy turned over, groaned and started to cry. As her voice sounded in her own throat, she screamed in terror at the strangeness. Rowenna hugged her, quilt and all, and patted her back and hummed. She seemed limp and lifeless, and a cold chill shot down Rowenna's back. Is she…? No, she has a fever. But she hurts. More tea? It was cold, now, but it should still work.She'd have to wake completely up or be strangled.

What to do…?

She drew the tiny body into her arms and rocked her back and forth. It would be nice to have a rocker, but this worked. The little girl seemed to relax. Reaching for the thermometer, she slipped it under her arm. Almost 103. Have to wake her up and sponge her face and arms. Mustn't hit 104.

"Nancy, sweetie? We have to cool your face and arms. Don't be scared. This will help you feel better in a little while." Rowenna hoped that was true.

The child opened tired eyes for a tiny slit and closed them and did not object to the cool cloth on her face, neck and arms. Neck was a mass of red and purple. Smell was terrible. Tomorrow's bath with soap would help. A little.

And so the night went. In the morning, Abe Parnell came quietly up the stairs. He smiled as he saw his little girl snugged in the arms of the nurse, both of them asleep. He waited long enough to see Nancy take a breath, then he was gone quietly. He'd done the right thing insisting on a fourteen-year-old as a nurse. An experienced nurse.

WALLY HOPKINS, GROCER EXTRAORDINAIRE

Wally was opening boxes of cans to put on the shelves of the WM. His box cutter must be wielded carefully to keep the boxes strong for another use. For the times he delivered orders, he needed the boxes again.

Placing the smaller boxes inside the ones a bit larger, he reduced the amount of space needed to store them. He rather liked this job, as it was active and yet took a bit of precision, and he liked storing them as compactly as possible. Another reason was that, by nature, he was a thrifty person and hated waste with what almost amounted to a passion.

It was a fact, actually, that he resented others doing this job, because they never did it as efficiently as he did. Then he grinned at himself over this little quirk. *Opening and storing boxes being a skill... I tell you!...* he chided himself with a chuckle. *Did I work hard in school for a job such as this...* and then, job completed, he went about making out the monthly charge statements for those (almost everyone) who preferred to buy by the month.

Then he realized he was just as careful with writing the numbers and correcting the totals as storing boxes. *Face it, Wally, you are just a careful person who enjoys attending to details. Surely this is the perfect job for you. Anyone could see that. Even God should be able to see that.* And Wally nodded in agreement with his own self.

He found he had a lot more thinking time, now that Rowenna managed to keep herself busy one or two hollows distant. Even Rowenna's best friend, Jewelee, was busy. That gave him a fair amount of alone time. Fact was... he didn't want alone time, because he didn't want to think.

Last week's marquee was nice and short, but that was no help. All it said was, "When the Lord guides, He provides." Now, why did he keep feeling like everything was directed at him?

But who else would it be for? Who else was trying to avoid being guided in any direction? Who was there that hated change as much as he? Sometimes he felt like Preacher Clemmons knew something he didn't know and was directing his marquee choices in that direction. That wasn't really fair... was it?

He took a quick trip down the center aisle of shelves and saw a bottle of peppersauce with the peach preserves he had just brought down from a cabin on Echo Mountain. Tiny little gray-haired Widow Harmon and her preserves sold like ice cream on a summer day.

Wally moved the bottle of peppersauce back where it belonged and picked up the broom and dustpan for the dirt tracked in the front door. He was just pushing the small accumulation out the front door when he came face to face with a young man with an armful of notices.

The bright face and pleasant voice asked, could he put a notice in their window?

Wally knew the answer to that. The WM did not allow notices in their window, but they provided a better place. A 4x6 size of valuable wall space was devoted to local ads. They were annotated for the date they were put up and allowed to stay… free… for a week. It was one of Wally's pick-up duties to check the dates and take down the ones that had used up their time.

The young man was pleased and accepted Wally's help with his flyer. Wally could not avoid reading what it said.

BIBLE STUDY COLLEGE, NEW IN BENTONVILLE. Come and join with us as we learn our way around God's direction for our lives. Contact Burle Smithfield for a space. Reasonably priced. This UNIQUE course offered for a limited time as a gift from a conference of churches.

Wally read it and groaned. That notice had to be there for a whole week, but why… really, why… would that be a problem to him? Why, he could rip it down as soon as the fellow cleared the doorway to the street. He could wad it up and toss it… and no one would be the wiser. No one but Wally himself.

The bulletin board was a popular place for customers to check out before picking up what they came for. There were comments. Like: 'Say, how much would a course like that cost?" and "Temporary for how long, I wonder?" Also, "What good is advertising way out here… at least fifty miles away?" with an answering comment from a fellow bystander, "The Frisco Railway goes right by it and it stops in Wishbone if we put out the flag."

Wally decided it was time to clean out the stalls and feed Mountain Minnie and the other three means of equine transportation. He passed by Miss Minnie and patted her long, brown face. She turned her eyes toward Wally, and it seemed to him she eyed him with sympathy.

He stroked her neck and told her she was a "Good Girl." And there came into his mind, purely and actively unbidden, the donkey who spoke with a human voice. *A man named Balaam wanted to go against God's direction, and God sent an angel to stop him, but he could not see the angel. Only his donkey saw the angel and stopped. Balaam beat him, but he would not face the angel blocking the way, and the donkey chided Balaam with a human voice.

Now, why did he have to think of that? God had not told him… Wally… to go somewhere that he had refused. He pushed away the memory of a commandment to study and 'when God guided, he provided'. He pushed and pushed, but the memory was still there.

Leaning his arm against the mare, he pushed his face onto Minnie's smooth, warm neck, and he felt the tears welling up in his eyes. Now, WHAT was going on? *Stop it this minute, Wally!* And then Wally sensed a grumble in Minnie's throat, and he felt her breath on his arm. She had looked around at him.

Swallowing, with difficulty, the lump in his throat, Wally looked up and asked, "Please, God, don't have Mountain Minnie talk to me. I know you can, but I would have a terrible time explaining it to myself. Getting bumped off the saddle by your angel was bad enough. I promise I will look and listen, and what you want me to do, I'll do. I ask one thing… may I wait until I'm eighteen and have the money to do what I have to do…so I don't have to worry about that?"

Mountain Minnie nibbled gently against his arm, then his belt, ending up at his pocket where he kept his handkerchief. Her mobile, rubbery lips sorted out the cloth and yanked. Wally felt the movement and jerked around. The horse pushed the cloth toward him with her conversational grumble. Hmmm, the trick Nathan taught her.

The dark eyes with the thick lashes continued to look at him with the sympathy and consolation. Wally nodded exaggeratedly at her and she responded with a nod of her own, a trick HE, Wally, had taught her when he first started making the mountain trips. He would say, "Are you ready?" and nod at her, and she would return the nod.

He fed the horses and returned to the store. When he went home today, the first thing to do would be to make a budget for the next two years. He wasn't sure his request for delay had been accepted, but he would act as though it was until he knew differently. The decision gave him a small amount of peace.

He had always been a person of plans, budgeting his time and, to a certain extent, saving his money. He really could not expect family help, nor would he ask. If God actually "guided," then it would be God's problem to "provide," wouldn't it?

God had seemed to take Rowenna away, and even Jewelee had her head set on a teaching certificate. Well, that gave him time, and maybe Granddad had some books around so he could be thinking about what would be required.

Above all, Wally loved to be prepared. Always had.

*Numbers, chapter 22: specifically verse 30.

BACK TO DEAD HORSE SPRINGS

Up on the mountain, things proceeded about as well as expected. Fever up and down, a shower of purple spots and a weary child. Being small, she seemed not to have the appetite she should, but Rowenna persevered.

Twice she helped Emily Parnell up the stairs to see her daughter. It was decided to keep the child there until the fever was over to avoid giving it to Abe Junior. Seemed to be successful.

The problem with little Abe, however, was that there was no one to entertain him while his sister was sick, and, more importantly, there was no one to tell on him when he was misbehaving. That was unfortunate.

There was Billy Goat, who had been a tiny, playful kid only months ago, and both children had fun playing with him. It was such fun when he butted his tiny head against their legs, and when they ran, they easily outran the little fellow. Their squeals and laughter seemed to egg him on to greater games.

But suddenly, it seemed, the tiny kid had horns and stood taller than their shoulders. It was decided that something would have to be done sometime before spring, and Big Abe was waiting for a storm, and when he couldn't work, he would turn the animal into food.

Meanwhile, the goat was to be tied, and the children were commanded to STAY AWAY from him. They must not even pick something from the garden to feed him, as they had been doing all summer. Why the parents thought a rope would hold a goat was a puzzle, as Big Abe had been around goats all his life. He knew a goat can eat anything, if properly motivated… and Billy Goat did not lack motivation.

The nannies made such small-sized, efficient sources of milk and cheese that a mountain farm must include them… and to have a fresh supply of milk, there had to be a billy. It was always possible to 'borrow' a neighbor's billy, but Big Abe thought he'd grow his own. He had forgotten the habits of a full-grown billy.

The creature had seen Emily Parnell heading for the clothesline with a bucket of wet clothes and was convinced that the bucket held some goodie meant for him. A good, solid butt produced only soggy clothing, and that irritated him… which was not hard to do.

To punish the human for fooling him, he took a run at her, and she might have avoided him if she were not in the last weeks of being 'in a family way'. Aiming his horns toward the stone ledge with a four-foot drop, he took a run and caught her on her left hip, raising her in the air and tossing her down the hill.

Purely amazing, it was, that she got only a broken foot and a lot of scrapes and a few black and blue spots. She had managed to crawl back to the ledge and somehow pull herself up. She wrapped, as well as she could, her foot and waited out the pain until Big Abe got home and could do a better job.

She should have, of course, seen a doctor and had it set, but that would have cost at least two whole days taking themselves and the children down to Eureka. If the mountain folk saw a doctor every time they needed to, nothing would ever get done. So she had resigned herself to the awkwardness of crutches and doing only what she positively had to do.

Young Nancy had been visiting her cousin in Eureka, excited that she would soon get to stay the week with her when school started. It would be impossible to get her all the way from Dead Horse Springss to either Wishbone or Eureka. So this was the next best thing to get her education.

Then the measles hit Eureka, climbing up the mountain to where the cousin lived, and the Parnells snatched their daughter home, but not soon enough.

That was when they had seen in the Cryer that Rowenna might be available, and they were purely happy about that. The fourteen-year-old proved to be forceful and efficient. Little Nancy soon began to improve.

She could now laugh with her pa when he climbed the stairs to see her, and if she had no mirror, she could not see how she looked. So far, Little Abe had not been near her and was strictly banned from the upstairs.

Now the little fellow must amuse himself. Mama was too slow getting things done to have any time for him, and the next best living thing was Billy Goat. Little Abe might have had trouble untying a rope, but after his ma's unfortunate incident, the animal was hooked to a chain.

Little Abe, being an average three-year-old, had no trouble at all with the metal hook that fastened the goat to a tree, and he promptly had himself a playmate. Billy Goat was totally willing and playfully swung his horns back and forth for the little fellow to clutch and try to hold.

Tired of that game, the goat remembered the fun of butting and took a carefully positioned run at the little boy. The horns met with only light resistance and the child went flying over the ledge and down the mountain toward Wishbone, landing fifteen feet down hill and sent rolling. Piercing screams went echoing across the valley and certainly into the upstairs windows.

Rowenna descended the stairs three steps at a time, landing on the floor just as Emily had levered herself into position at the door. The girl passed the woman in full speed and headed for the ledge and the screams. Leaping down and crawling through the bushes and briers, she reached for the boy and saw no great amount of blood.

Somehow, that encouraged her. Reaching him, she tested arms and legs, and lifting his shoulders brought no louder protests, so she scooped him up in her arms and crawled back through the undergrowth.

By now Emily reached the edge of the ledge but could not, of course, offer help in getting him back up. Rowenna sat the child of the edge of the ledge and fiercely commanded, "Sit and don't move!" He did… screaming at the top of his very healthy lungs.

Hoisting herself onto the ledge, she gathered up the child and headed for the kitchen. He was still producing agonized screams, so there must still be something wrong. He was finally able to thrust a hand toward Rowenna and point to it with the other hand.

Emily took over. Carefully manipulating his fingers, she settled on the thumb, creating piercing agony. A thumb that should not have bent that way.

Meanwhile, Rowenna had been examining legs and feet and was relieved to see him sitting straight, though she had absolutely no experience for anything remotely resembling this.

Emily prepared cold water and tried to make him hold his hand in the water to avoid swelling. No avail. Nothing to do but wait for Big Abe, who seemed to have some skill with first aid. Rowenna searched her brain and could only come up with willow bark tea, which eased pain… to some degree… and encouraged relaxation.

Young Abe did not want to drink tea… he'd rather scream.

Rowenna suddenly remembered her upstairs patient and dashed up the stairs. Nancy was a sodden lump hiding under the covers, and when Rowenna peeled them back, she was met with teary blue eyes and the solemn statement, "I know my brother's dead." Then a hopeful post script, "Isn't he?"

Rowenna pulled the child to her lap and hugged her. (Hugs were not in the book as part of a remedy, but they seemed to be called for here.) "No, sweetie, no. He couldn't cry like that if he was dead, so you don't need to worry. He only hurt his thumb, and your pa can fix it when he comes home." She hoped that was true.

Nancy was taking liquids well, now, and could get herself to the chamber pot that was very close to the bed. Rowenna went to the kitchen to get juice for her and then encourage her to sleep for a while. She reached the kitchen to see Little Abe sitting the floor, now contemplating his swelling thumb, and Emily on a chair bent double.

Fear grabbed Rowenna's lungs and paralyzed her feet. She stopped in mid-step and stared from the swollen thumb to the groaning woman, knowing she must get control of her thinking. There was something that must be done.

The most horrifying thing she saw was the widening pool of moisture under the chair, spreading around the chair legs and outward toward Emily's shoes. Unbelievingly, she blinked… so the pool would disappear… but instead, it widened.

She hurriedly poured juice into the glass with a shaking hand, placed the pitcher back on the cabinets and sprinted up the stairs. Handing the glass to the little girl, she whispered (remembering to smile with reassurance), "Sweetie, I want you to drink this and take a good long nap so you'll feel better when your pa comes to see you."

Nancy nodded understanding and began to drink. Rowenna gave her a final smile and waved. "I'll be back after while."

Downstairs, she poked her head into a closed door and saw the crib, obviously used as a bed. Picking up the three-year-old, she hugged him and rocked him in her arms as she took him to the room. "It's time for a little sleep so your hand will be better. I'm going to shut the door, so you must be very quiet." She reinforced the command with a finger over her lips. A pair of solemn brown eyes followed her, sniffing and hiccoughing softly.

As promised, Rowenna shut the door, and silence remained within. Now for Emily. Straightening up with difficulty, Emily turned pathetic eyes toward the fourteen-year-old 'nurse'. "Honey, I'm so sorry, but I…."

Rowenna butted in. "I know. Can you go to your bed?"

She nodded. "But I'm not ready for the bed, and there isn't time."

"No time…?"

"No, honey. You must…" She cringed, waiting for the contraction to pass. "Help me quickly. Spread a folded sheet on the rug. I'll show… you in the bedroom."

In the bedroom, Emily pointed to a chest. "Bottom drawer… Midwife box… ready. Bring… let me lay on floor. Bed too soft… Spread sheet here."

Rowenna obeyed and spread the snowy sheet on the multicolored rag-rug. More instructions.

"Scissors handy. Tie threads… I can't…" And she groaned pathetically from intense pain. "Honey… I'm sorry, but… you must be ready. Now."

"Ready...?"

"Yes. Help me with my clothes and hurry. Don't try... to keep from hurting me... Just hurry."

Rowenna hurried. Underclothing. Shoes. Stockings. All the time struggling to dredge from her memory the words she had read just last night in an attempt to make herself sleepy.

"Now, honey. It's now..." and a prolonged, pathetic groan filled the room and ended in an eerie shriek. Seconds strung out like hours as Rowenna wrung her shaking hands and mentally begged for instruction from the suffering woman. From the angel. From anyone...!

Popping into her head was the statement she had heard so many times from grown-up women under a variety of circumstances. "Babies come when babies come, and there ain't no stoppin' 'em." The girl soon saw that the statement was true.

Somehow, there in her hands was a tiny pink baby doll, perfect for a little girl's Christmas present. Swallowing hard, she looked at the baby in her hands and at the woman on the floor.

"Honey... listen. Tie string... next to me, and again next to ba... baby. Can you...?"

"Uh... yes." And the words from the book came back to her like newsprint on her mind. Wrap twice. Tie twice. Clip between. Wrap baby with binder to keep tie in place. She wrapped and tied... and clipped.

She looked at Emily. "Binder...?"

Emily managed to answer, "Basket...."

And there was the thick band of cloth, looking just like the picture in the book. A lot of fourteen-year-old girls would have known about most of these things, but a thirteen kid, being the last of the litter, had no one to observe.

Wrapping the strap around the tiny tummy, she carefully avoided the flapping arms and small legs, drawing themselves up at the knees. Good job. Picking up one of the soft flannel towels, she wrapped the little thing as she would have a doll, resisting the urge to hug her.

Emily again. "Basket for baby... behind bed. Then... Come back. I need..." Another groan.

Rowenna jerked upward. Holding the wrapped baby, who was now screaming her own indignation at entering the harsh world. Tucking her in the bassinette, she looked to Emily for further instructions.

"My... uh, stomach. Push...."

A vigorous shake of the head. Never! NEVER! This poor lady had been through enough.

But Emily insisted. "You have to, honey. I'll help what I can. There's more to come...?"

Rowenna was horrified. Another baby...? It couldn't be, there was only one bassinette. Besides....

"NOW!" demanded Emily. "Push my belly button down."

Rowenna obeyed, and the horror of what happened next would make nightmares for the rest of her life... she was sure.

"Wrap it up in sheet. See bucket in corner... put there."

She did. Then she knelt beside Emily for further direction. "Rowenna, my dear, you did an excellent job. I'm so terribly tired now. Just let me rest for an hour. Can you clean baby? Soft clothes... basket."

"I can help you onto the... bed...?"

Shake of the head. "No. Just let me lie here. Can you light a fire and make me some tea...? Chamomile, if you can find it."

Rowenna heaved a relieved sigh. THAT... she could do with confidence. There had been no sound from either child... *oh, thank you, Angel. It has to have been you who quieted them.* She picked up the bassinette basket and a soft cloth and retired to the kitchen.

The baby's skin seemed so thin and delicate, Rowenna was afraid of puncturing her, but she did her best. Face and ears... the book had said. Turn baby face down and hold... maybe clear throat. Obviously there was nothing wrong with this baby's throat, so she ignored that and returned the basket to the bedroom.

Emily's eyes were closed, and she seemed out of pain. Rowenna climbed the stairs high enough to see that Nancy was quiet. From the kitchen, she heard nothing behind the closed door.

As quietly as possible, she laid a fire and brought in a fresh pail of water. Emily's cupboard was neatly arranged, and the chamomile was right beside the dandelion. Imagine… keeping your garden tea in alphabetical rows.

The kettle steamed, and Rowenna found the peppermint tea. Shaking a bit in a mug, she filled it with water. Lovely steam swirled up and Rowenna moved her face into the fragrant vapor. It was done, and she had lived through it. *That has got to mean something, and when I have time, I'll try to learn what it was.* The peppermint tea was a warm comfort in her stomach. Then a bit of hunger growled. Food. Supper. Someone would be coming in very hungry. What could she do to help?

Cornmeal. Eggs. Beans had been put to soak but did not have time to cook. Potatoes. A ham bone with bits of meat on it… obviously meant for the beans. She put it in a kettle and covered with hot water. It was going to be ham gravy for the potatoes. The beans could just fend for themselves. What else….

Eggs… of course…! Where were they…? She found them in a basket hanging on the porch and lifted an even dozen of them into a kettle and covered them with water. There was mustard. If she could just find an onion. Maybe still in the garden. Egg salad went with everything.

A brisk breeze had sprung up, so she tossed a coat around her shoulders. Big Abe's coat. Smelled like the woodland. Garden behind the fence, and there were the onion tops bent over as they should be. She pulled three. She liked a lot of onion in her egg salad.

Nearby she could hear the nanny goats baaing to be milked, but she decided she couldn't take that on. She'd never milked a goat in her life. Enough was enough, but at least she was now on familiar ground. She had not much experience in the kitchen, but she could throw something together. She thought Big Abe would have little to complain about when he saw the baby. So thoughtful of the little thing to go to sleep for a while.

The hour was up, and she poured hot water over the chamomile tea. Tiptoed into the room. No need. Mama was on the bed with the little girl in her lap. She smiled her contentment and reached for the tea. No wonder the baby was so quiet… she was busy with her own supper.

A racket outside brought a look of alarm on Emily's face. "He's early! I hope nothing…" She couldn't bear to express her fear in words… she'd had enough for the day. Rowenna also hoped… enough had gone wrong already.

Big Abe came through the door, paused and looked around, then on into the bedroom. Staring from one to the other, he sighed with relief and his tense shoulders relaxed.

"Left the woods a little early. Needed to see how you were."

"Come look at your little girl."

Rowenna slipped away and continued with the meal, peeling the eggs from their shells and chopping the onions.

Later, she tried to remember the evening and couldn't. Somehow things got done. The thumb was splinted and the children fed. The milk was taken care of. The family loved milk, and that filled out the meal quite nicely. Nancy had no fever, so she was also permitted milk. It made a good liquid as well.

The next morning, Big Abe had planned to stay at home, but Emily insisted Rowenna was doing fine, and she'd be able to help a little. She could take care of little Susan.

Rowenna stayed another ten days and left Dead Horse Springss two days after Christmas. Interesting that the holiday had passed over without much fanfare except for a book of the Christmas story for Nancy and a toy wagon for the boy… one his pa had made.

Abe Parnell took her home in the buggy… a silent trip across the ridge until they headed down into the valley of Wishbone.

"Miss Rowenna, one of the best things I ever did was come for you to help. I can only think the angels directed me to look at the classifieds, because I seldom do. I have nothing to sell and need to buy nothing, but I read it and learned that you had been on a nursing call and that you were home. You did an unbelievable job this last month, and Emily wants to give Susan your name in the middle to remember you by… not that we would ever forget you."

Rowenna swallowed hard and sought for good words… but found none. She rode along with thoughts and words swirling in her head, but none of them went together. She had to get to Granddad and get them straightened out. She was not yet ready to trust her own feelings.

As they pulled into the yard at the hilltop house, the man handed her a small drawstring bag heavy with what seemed to be coins. She looked at him and shook her head. She did not work for money.

He pushed it back toward her and said, "I know. Your pa told me you did not hire out, but we get to give you a gift. Open the bag and look, and see how much we appreciated you."

She opened the bag and counted ten silver dollars. Wide-eyed and heart pounding, she looked back at him.

He nodded. "But you were worth ten times that much. You even missed Christmas with your family." Then he came in the house with her and talked with Ma and Pa, but she heard nothing of what was said. She disappeared into her room and fell face down on her bed, tears flowing.

"Now, WHAT is going on with that...? Stop it, I say..." she chided herself firmly, and finally the tears stopped.

She was at home. She still had a nest to return to... and had not yet flown out on her own. She was clearly not ready to fly. She had done nothing to be praised for but only what was in front of her to be done... and she had been scared spitless ninety-nine percent of the time. And she was good at figuring percents and fractions.

Home, at last. The nest... but not for long. The baby birds eventually got too big for the nest. And girls...? Well, Laverne had gone from home at almost seventeen. Jadeen had been working for a year. But for herself, there was tonight... and tomorrow night... that she still had the nest. And tomorrow she had Granddad.

A movement on the bed. Ma. First a hand on her arm, and then a stroke along her cheek. She sat up, and Ma put an arm around her shoulder. More tears.

"Ma... I can't."

"But, darling, you already did."

"NO! I shook like a leaf, and the little girl was so sick. And here I was telling her mother what to do. I should not have done that. The little girl was so sweet and did everything I asked. I put short socks on her hands because she scratched in her sleep. She called them 'sock-mittens'.

"I told long stories to put her to sleep and rocked her in my arms when she cried. I know she wanted her ma, but the stairs were so difficult and narrow she couldn't climb without help, and I could hardly help her up. The little girl wanted milk, but I couldn't... oh, Ma... I can't."

"Can't what...?"

"I was scared. I thought I might do something wrong. I was all alone."

"You were not alone."

"Yeah, I know. God, of course."

"More than that, my dear. On your third day, Pa was there, and Mr. Parnell said you were doing 'famously'. That was his word for how you did. I liked the sound of it. Then Granddad was there three times... just to make certain you were safe and not needing to be brought home."

"But, Ma, I didn't see them! Not one time for even a peek and a couple of words."

"They didn't want you to see them."

"But why...?"

"If you saw them, you might come home before the job was done, and you would regret it all your life. Also, and more important, you might think that we didn't trust you to do your best, and if you saw Granddad, you might believe we thought you couldn't do it... then you likely couldn't. You needed to know what you could do."

Ma took a hanky from her apron pocket. It smelled of the lye soap from the wash... a comfortingly clean smell. Rowenna sniffed and wiped her eyes. Ma continued.

"My little one, my thirteenth kid, I'm proud of you. Today you are frightened of what you already did, and this might happen to you all your life... but this I know. Frightened or not, you will finish what you start. Also, you are able to listen to your better sense and act quickly when you have to. We heard how you rescued the little boy from the brambles."

"But Ma, Emily could hardly walk around the kitchen. She couldn't have gotten him."

"But you could, and you did. Not only that, you helped with the baby. We were told that she would have had a very difficult time if you had not been there. Labor starting and both children ill? Think about it. Once more, you were in the right place to do what you could do."

Rowenna looked at Ma. Carefully LOOKED at her. Wrinkles forming around her eyes and mouth. Lovely wrinkles. They gave a friendly design to her face. She could imagine a mother in no other way… each of the thirteen had left a furrow of concern on her face. That meant a lot of furrows. The last born. Thirteenth kid. The tag end of what was already a full and complete family. And Ma still had enough love to wrap around her.

Ma continued. "We always, your pa and me, tried to let you children do what you had to do. Your older sisters looked forward to marriage, but our last three were very different. We tried to understand that and let Laverne leave on her own… much before we wanted to, but she knew where she wanted to go, and we made ourselves let her.

"Jadeen got the job she wanted from pure determination and making a nuisance of herself. She works hard to prove herself important… and seems to be succeeding. And now you want to go in another direction, and Granddad is certain you will figure out the way when you're ready. Pa and I want that for you, and it seemed that the Parnells' was a perfect place for you to see for yourself if that kind of service was for you."

They sat in silence for a full minute. "So now I want you to rest a while, and I'll call you for supper. What would you like to eat?"

Oh, what lovely words! "I'd like one of those sweet potatoes that are so orange they're almost red. Boiled, sliced and fried with bacon. And I'd like cornmeal flapjacks on the side. And onions. Sliced thick."

Ma smiled, rearranging all her facial wrinkles into a wonderful pattern of pleasure. "You have it! Now, stretch out on the bed and rest. I'll call you."

Ma eased out the door, and Rowenna sighed contentedly, stretching out on her soft, soft bed with a mattress of goose feathers. So soft… just like a nest… and she was asleep.

TWO LETTERS

It was morning, and Ma let her enjoy her scrambled eggs and biscuits. Then, "You missed Christmas with the family, but I saved you a slice of Aunt Ramona's lemon cake and two pieces of the fruit cake you like, thick with chinky pins and candied orange peel. Have them when you want them."

Then, almost as a second thought, "And there were two letters for you. Jewelee and the nursing school in Memphis."

"The school…?" But she picked up the note from her friend first.

> … and my test comes up in three weeks over in Bentonville. My folks say there's no one to go with me, and if you are available and willing, they will buy your train ticket, and you can share my room for the night. They think two girls will be safe together. Can you come?
>
> I'll be at the church Sunday, and you can let me know. This is terribly important, and I've studied so hard, and you're the only one Ma will trust. If you can't go with me, then I'll have to wait another year. Please! Pretty please! You're the only one, so can you do that for me? If you will, I promise I'll be there to do something for you when you need it.

She did not realize how soon that would happen.

The note sounded like "pure Jewelee"… enthusiastic and dramatic but also flattering. Good friend. The girls had stood in for each other ever since they met in the first grade.

Turning to Ma, she explained, "Jewelee needs someone to go to Bentonville with her for her test. Her folks will pay my way." Then she picked up the other letter.

> Dear Miss Moffat,
>
> We received your 'thank you' letter with pleasure and appreciation. We truly wish we could help you more, but this is what we decided we could do. We do not require our students to buy the expensive books, but we just add a small amount to their tuition to let them borrow them.
>
> That, however, will not work for you, so we are sending you the name of the publisher and a list of the books we use for the course. They are very nicely bound and will

look good on any bookshelf, and are also good for future reference should you pursue this avenue.

We thought that if you managed the price of the books and truly took the time to study them, we could do something else for you. When you finish and feel you are ready for the test, you may furnish us with two responsible, older persons in your town, and we will send those persons the test to administer to you. This will not, of course, furnish you a license, but you can be 'certified', and the absence of a license should not stop you from performing services to those in need. Passing the test is sure to give you the confidence you will appreciate.

In the four years before you are eighteen, there may be changes that make your efforts easier. This is certainly a growing need, and there are many young ladies like you waiting to fill it. It takes so long to be a doctor, and they cannot be everywhere, so that makes nurses even more valuable. Scattered populations such as are in parts of our country will benefit greatly from young ladies such as you. In closing, Miss Moffat, we say that it has been a pleasure to hear from you, and we sincerely hope this plan is something you can manage.

Our best wishes,

Nursing School

Memphis, Tennessee

She read the letter to herself, then out loud to her waiting parents. She handed Pa the list naming the books and the prices. The total was a whopping $9.80! Just for books!

Rowenna asked, "Ma, how much is a money order?"

"Hmmm, well, it depends on the amount involved, but I think about twenty cents."

Somehow she was not surprised and went to her room for the little bag with the appreciation gift of $10.00. All of it well-earned in fear and trembling, if not in knowledge and skill.

"I'll go see Granddad, and he'll help me with the order. If it's all right with you two." And she was gone, looking forward to the walk down to Main Street. The leaves were off the trees, all except the black-jack oaks, and it seemed she could see forever. As she left the Moffat property, the church came into view. It looked like a little figure for a Christmas village decoration when the eastern sun shone on the beautiful windows… the ones that cousin Wally had earned clawing through the waters of Little Mulberry.

Today was the twenty-ninth day of December, 1914. Granddad was found on Main Street, seated on the 'spit and whittle' bench with six other old men. The subject under discussion was the unrest in Europe with the royalty squabbling together and the attempted assassinations. The squabbles of royalty so often resulted in the bloodshed of peasants as they struggled over the ownership of land. The old men nodded and agreed… what was the world coming to? And it was good that it would not affect America. The sad thing was that they did not know what the next five years would bring… all the way to Wishbone!

Seeing his granddaughter, Granddad left the men and the bench and took her to the indoor diner that served wonderful tea, cookies and sandwiches.

Seated with her tea, she began, "Granddad, I truly did not ask my angel to bring a message that would be an absolute answer. I really did not get that far, because I knew I was not important enough, but now I want you to see what I got in the mail… and as a gift from Mr. Parnell."

She pushed the list of books across the tiny tea-table, put the drawstring bag on it and proceeded to read the letter in low, almost whispered words. She hardly believed it was real, and if she spoke normally, it might evaporate into thin air. Granddad listened silently.

When she finished, he asked, "Rowenna, my treasure, have you read the newest marquee your cousin did without you? He even had to have the Carpenter Shop make more letters, and he pushed them really snug, but they're all there."

Rowenna shook her head. "Haven't had time, Granddad. I haven't even had time to look at the Cryer and see what Jadeen published about me."

Granddad slid a worn copy of the periodical toward her, and she read… fitted in among the buying and selling… these words.

> This week's church marquee: "Delight thyself in the Lord, and He will give thee the desires of thine heart. Psa 37:4."

It was a bit more than she could manage, so she stared out the window at the shoppers passing by, taking advantage of the lovely December weather that occasionally happens in the northern part of Arkansas. To relieve the tension, Granddad touched her arm and said, "Read this."

Tucked between the ads was this informative note.

> Some of us felt there would be those in Wishbone wondering what was the latest with the Girl with the Gun. Well, she's back home, having royally tested herself for a family up in Dead Horse Springss.Measles, broken bones and a brand new citizen of Arkansas. She ably took care of it all, and the new little girl carries her name. It seems there is nothing too difficult for my sister, and she didn't even have to use her gun!

Rowenna grinned at the extravagance, and Granddad suggested, "Does that or does that not sound like your sister is secretly proud of you?"

"No, Granddad. She only likes having something to write that's so different that people will notice her. It would be the same if I shot up the bank and took off with the funds."

It was Granddad's turn to grin. "You could be right. Are you here to make that order, or do you want to think about it? Ten dollars is a lot of money to spend so quickly."

"Oh, I must make the order. That's why God gave me the opportunity, and he even made the pennies come out even with what I really wanted."

"Now, what makes you think that?"

"My angel whispered it in my ear on the way down here. Who else would know exactly how much money I needed to buy what I wanted when I didn't even know how much it would take? I want to do it now... this minute... if you're finished with your tea."

In her mind, she played out the timeline. A week to get there and two weeks for the package to come. Just about the time Jewelee took her test.

Order made, she left him to stop in on the Thimbles and Spools and release him back to the 'spit and whittle' to help the other fellows cure the ills of the world.

"One last question, Granddad. Is there really a difference from the desires of the head and those of the heart?"

The old man paused for a moment of thought. "I'm thinking that would be for you to figure out."

OUTFITTING THE GIRL WITH THE GUN

The fourteen-year-old girl walked away from the Post Office of Wishbone Hollow with a confusing feeling of being filled up and also empty. It seemed to be the end of a paragraph of the story of her life, and it had ended with the 'ball and bat' of the exclamation point.

It was done. The books would come, and they would work for her, or they would not. It was just something that must be done... like gathering the chinky pins or climbing trees for the muscadine grapes. Or caring for her sister or the tiny girl on the side of the mountain. She was the one who was there and, at the time, the only one who could do what she did.

After a month of not seeing her, the aunts were overjoyed. Aunt Sophrenia was the loudest. "I told you all that she would come today. Didn't I...? I said it first minute I knew she was home. Good thing, too, cause...."

"Let someone else get a word in edgewise, can't you? She don't belong just to you."

"Honey, we needed you to try out the little... well, we call it a pocket, but it's really a...."

"Holster! It was me that was brave enough to say that a pocket for a gun was a holster, be it on fellow or girl or on a horse!"

"Give 'er a chance to take a breath, will you? She hasn't even had no tea."

"Rowenna, sweetie… we have something new that we think may help you carry your gun. We may need to make changes, but…."

"She can tell us what she needs. Let's get with it, and then she can have cinnamon apple cake and tea. Where did you put it, Soph…?"

"Didn't put it nowhere. It's right here in my hand. We was thinkin', the others and me, that if we can get this to fit your waist, it'll hide under any skirt that has gathers, and you're too young for those ugly straight skirts."

And there it was in her hand. Created from white broadcloth, it had a narrow belt for a waistband, and it crinkled gently from the elastic insert. Immediately hanging down was a pocket the exact shape of her 22mm Winchester.

"Havin' this under your skirt and high up to your waist should make it handy to get to if you need it in a hurry. Course, that'd mean liftin' your skirt, but there wouldn't be no floppin' about like if it was in a pocket."

Cecelia was not to be left out. "The thing to remember is to have a decent pettislip on all the time, so if it shows, it won't be indecent. We made a pettislip for you to look at to see how it would work."

And there they stood, the three dear ladies, each face with wrinkles exaggerated by concern. Sophrenia held the 'holster', lovingly caressing the smoothness of their stitches. No trimming as they would have liked, but just plain white broadcloth, doubled and quilted together attractively.

It was solidly attached to the belt and would not, as Aunt Georgiana had pointed out, 'flop about'. And Rowenna agreed that the current design did 'flop about' when she hurried.

Cecelia held up the pettislip. Soft blue and flared slightly, it was bordered at the hem with a softly-pleated ruffle edged in tatted lace. Quite discreet and understated. Actually a marvelous creation! The fourteen-year-old girl desired it immediately and with all her heart.

There it was… not fussy with decoration, but shapely and functional and very feminine… classy might be the appropriate word.

The excitement of the ladies was almost palpable as they studied her face to anticipate her reaction. So quickly they'd changed their attitude on weaponry if it involved the life of their beloved girl.

Aunt Sophrenia gathered the conversation back by saying, "Now, this pettislip is only for a pattern. We'd need to make several when we see how this works. It will be more discreet if you have to lift your skirt and the pettislip matches, somewhat. Do you see…?"

She clearly saw… and immediately stripped out of her pettislip and reached for the new creation, and the dainty, lady-like Jewelee, whose dream was teaching the city's children… someday… when the opening occurred. She'd tried to interest Rowenna to join with her until Rowenna pointed out that only one of them would be selected if an opening came, and who would it be…?

She pulled the garment smoothly on… over her drawers. Waist fit was perfect. The holster circled her waist with the elastic band and the very feminine gun pocket. Fit beautifully.

She looked at the watching three and grabbed them all, in turn, and hugged them. "Oh, I love you so much, and you are so good to me. I just love it so much, and my skirt hides it perfectly."

Aunt Cecelia tweaked the gathers here and there and tilted her head to view her critically. Nodding her satisfaction, she asked, "Are there any changes you'd like?"

Should she? It was so new to them and they were so proud, but she knew she'd say it sooner or later. Might as well be now. "I love this dearly. In addition, I would like to have the holster attached to the waist of the pettislip on one, maybe… two of the pettislips…?"

Aunt Georgiana squared her shoulders. "Now, you will remember that I suggested that and was voted down. That would make less bulk around her waist, and the holster could possibly come loose and fall off, but a lady never loses her pettislip. And there's something else I thought of. On one or two outfits, maybe, we could make the pettislip from the same fabric as the skirt and then it would be nigh onto impossible to be indiscreet."

When Aunt Georgiana had a point to make, she made it, leaving nothing to doubt.

She was served tea and the cinnamon apple cake, a favorite since she was a toddler. The four of them sat at the table and ate, but the conversation shifted to a three-way conference on what fabrics should be used, and should they maybe order something from Montgomery Ward Catalog? There'd be time, wouldn't there, honey?

Rowenna let them plan. It was their favorite thing to do, and one thing was certain, the final product would be something she would like very much and would bring a tolerant smile from Ma.

On your first little girls, you wanted to dress them yourself, but on the thirteenth kid… well, you do the figuring. Free clothing and happy relatives added up to something, didn't it?

Late afternoon she stopped at the WM. Wally was joyous to see her. The siblings of the pair were older and went their own ways, but these two could have been practically joined at the hip for their likes and tolerances and their need for the approval of each other.

"Hang around a while, and we can do the new marquee. I've only got an hour to go here."

She amused herself at the sheet of cork that served as a bulletin board. It was always interesting, and maybe even more so than the Classified Ads.

The word 'Bentonville' popped out at her. Three weeks and she would get to ride the train over there, stay the night and ride back. Definitely something to be looking forward to.

Hmmm, Bible study? In a game…? Was that like church or maybe something different? She'd never thought of the Bible to be a book to be 'studied'. Maybe she'd looked at it wrong. That would be something to think about.

And later she stood in the churchyard by the sign holding the letter box. A little one this time, and maybe just as well. The south was picking up a frisky breeze and was barreling down Echo Mountain with it. She shivered a little in her light jacket.

When the sign was finished, they stood back and smiled. It said, "Good, minus God, leaves an 'o'. Nothing. Think about it."

And by mutual decision, they strolled over to the Thimbles and Spools for hot chocolate before they split and headed up the hills to their homes.

BENTONVILLE, ARKANSAS, 1914

The cousins sat in comfortable silence at the round kitchen table in the Thimbles and Spools, dunking their marshmallows under the hot chocolate made with cream.

The three ladies in residence were discussing the pettislip-holster design. Should the holster be a separate item attached at the waist to the slip, or should it be applied as a pocket... as one in a piece with the garment... and should it be made with the same fabric... The pair at the table thought nothing of the argument. Common thing. It seemed they actually liked this sort of thing.

The pocket all of a piece seemed to be winning, but Rowenna was of the opinion that details being discussed by others were just details she could ignore. There was something else that she did not ignore.

Turning to the young man beside her, she demanded, "What's wrong with you?"

"Nothing."

"That's not true. Something's on your mind. What is it?"

"Nothing, I tell you."

"Alright, John Wallace Hopkins. Be that way if you insist, but in the end, you'll tell me, so it needs to be now, so I don't keep bugging you."

"Aw... lay off. Why do you think you need to know everything?"

"Not everything... just what's bugging you. Something wrong at the WM?" That seemed to be a good place to start.

Shake of the head. Sip of chocolate. Then he turned to look at her. "Just stop prying. You'll know sometimes."

"I want to know now. You act like it has something to do with that marquee sign."

"No, not that one. I like that one."

"Then which one? Are you tired of letting me pick the letters?"
Shake of the head.

"Is it something Preacher Clemmons did... or said...?"

"Oh, hush and drink your chocolate. It's going to be cold climbing up that hill to get home."

"I'm not going home until I find out what's wrong with you. So tell me which sign has you bothered, so I can shut up."

"You'll think it's silly."

"How will that be different from usual? A lot of things you say are silly. I like silly things."

"ALRIGHT! It was that one while you were gone that said 'Study to show yourself approved'."

"Oh! I know that one, and the rest of it says to do that so you will be worth what you're paid. What's wrong with that?"

"I think I'm going to have some studying to do."

"Huh, well, I know about someone else who'll be studying. We can study together."

"No. It's not that kind. You know how they say Granddad had to do a lot of studying to be able to preach? And Preacher Clemmons just came out of school seven years ago. That kind of studying."

Silence, and Rowenna nodded. "Preach! You think you're goin' to have to preach! How do you know?"

"I'd tell you if I knew, but it keeps raising its head up inside me. I keep pushing it down, but it seems to be winning."

"What's your head sayin' to do?"

"Maybe to just get ready and don't be surprised when it happens. But listen, don't you ever tell anyone. It may go away."

"I won't tell, but sooner or later, everyone will know."

The chocolate was gone, and the pair of cousins parted to go to their homes. Rowenna had something to think about all the way to the hilltop. Somehow it didn't seem to be a surprise about Wally, and she thought God had made a good choice, if indeed it was God, and not just a touch of the flu or something else that had Wally concerned.

It was on Sunday that Rowenna could see Jewelee.

For the last months, the girls had rarely seen each other because of Jewelee having her nose firmly in the book, learning and re-learning things she already knew.

The fact was, for these two girls to have been long-time friends, the chances were infinite and astronomical. Total opposites in so many areas with visions of the future in totally different realms. They were, however, both motivated, hard-headed and determined, as well as having a clear goal ahead, if they could just get to it. The other thing they had in common was an understanding of each other and the other's fierce determination that the other should get what she wanted.

Jewelee could hardly contain herself for the excitement, much less listen to the exhortation from the pulpit. Only three weeks… and would she actually be ready for the test?

She whispered, "Papa said be sure you took your gun." Rowenna nodded reassurance. She was accustomed to her friend's nervousness. Where Jewelee only fought nervousness, Rowenna had more difficulty with figuring out her own particular direction.

After ordering the books, Rowenna could relax a bit, because there was nothing to do until they came… and then SHE would be the one with her nose in the books. Such was the problem of growing up.

On January 22, they were put on the train by Jewelee's papa, also chattering nervously to cover his apprehension. His daughter would be going miles away and would live or die by her performance. Enough to make any papa jittery.

A packed lunch was in the basket. "Mama said don't eat nothin' but cookies before goin' in. She thinks I might…."

"I know. And you probably would. I, however, get the ham sandwich and the two boiled eggs, as well as cookies. I'm never too nervous to eat."

While her friend stared out the train window, busy being nervous, Rowenna replayed her thought of the last few days.

She had the wonderful new skirt the color of Little Mulberry River on a sunshiny dawn. Blue. Deep and dark, a little darker than royal blue. The color was chosen carefully by the aunts as one that would not show the soil and grime of travel by rail and allow her to appear at the end of the line in acceptable condition.

Moreover, the pettislip was made of the same fabric… fitting modestly over her legs and capably hiding the gun holster, attached smoothly as any handkerchief pocket. The outer skirt sported a lightly gathered ruffle allowing ease in walking while maintaining feminine gracefulness. It had taken many words among the three, but the end product was something all three could agree was perfection and just when she needed it for this important trip.

They arrived in Bentonville at 8:30, and the test was at ten. An hour and a half to check into their room and freshen up. Jewelee's hands shook so bad she could not comb her hair. No matter… Rowenna was there.

The test-takers were locked in a room by themselves, and the companions were sent away with instruction not to come back for seven hours as the students would be served lunch cloistered together. Rowenna hoped her friend would not be forced to eat.

So now she had seven hours to explore the huge town of Bentonville. So exciting. Unconsciously, she patted her right hip where the 22mm rested, loaded and ready.

She walked three blocks straight ahead, and three blocks to the right. Such wonders in every direction. Everything in the world was on sale here. Interesting items were displayed in the windows.

She had just turned the corner to return, being careful not to get lost, when she saw the interesting sign across the street. Crossing over on the brick street, she saw that the sign said exactly what she thought it said.

DID YOU KNOW? THE BIBLE IS THE MOST INTERESTING BOOK IN THE WORLD. It covers a longer time span than any other, and it deals with the natural and the supernatural. It tells of dozens of humans who obeyed and also those who disobeyed their better senses, and a number of humans who actually arose from the dead.

It tells of water burning,* iron floating,** a whirlwind carrying a person to another world.3* There's a story of a never-failing barrel of meal,4* and a cruise of oil that multiplied hundreds of times.5* It speaks of a man being fed by birds,6* and a river parting on command.7*

If that is not enough, learn about a man whose bones retained enough power to bring a dead man back to life,8* and these happenings involve only two prophets who were friends. Come in and check us out!

"I really shouldn't go in there," Rowenna told herself. The truth of it was, however, that Rowenna did not listen. This was one puzzle that surely had an answer, and she had enough of the other kind. She knew of the Bible as a friend and a guide, but not an interesting book to read just as a story.

She met a friendly face. So far, so good. "Sir, I came across the street to read your sign, and I have a question. Is there some special way of reading that makes the book interesting?"

"Young lady, what a wonderful question. To answer it, this is a Bible Study Course that is more fun than any game you ever played. It starts with a story on the first three sessions, and then for every story thereafter, there are games involving quotations, occupations, miracles, punishments and a lot of other categories. It is best played in a group of a dozen to a dozen and a half. There are a lot of varieties among the rules, and each leader is encouraged to create his own additional games."

Rowenna listened and stared at the material before her. Squares of pasteboard of many colors and playing boards.

Encouraged by her interest, the young man continued, "The object and aim of this course is to create a familiarity and friendship with the Bible so it will actually be used for information and even pleasure, instead of being allowed to collect dust on a shelf. Would you possibly be able to come?"

A quick shake of the head. "No, because I live out in Wishbone and couldn't get here. But it surely sounds interesting." She looked up, smiling sadly.

The man returned her smile. "In that case, we move over to plan B. The whole course comes as a kit and may be purchased. We require the purchaser to come in and be willing to give us an hour to receive a beginning explanation. Anyone can be part of the study, and even children of 10 and 12 years old have fun with it. Does this sound like something you could do?"

A sigh and shake of the head. "It wouldn't be for me, sir, but I have a cousin who really needs this. He's facing a course of study and he's dreading it. He doesn't much like to study."

"How old is he?"

"Past sixteen. He's really smart... he just likes to do other things."

The man nodded. "Don't we all. That's why this is called a game, because it plays like a game. Let me give you some additional literature, and if you can persuade him to come, we guarantee it will not be a waste of time."

"I'll try, sir." She took the packet and thanked him. Could this possibly be the answer for Wally? Maybe Preacher Clemmons could use it. Anyway, she'd take it along.

Rowenna had lunch in a diner. Maybe not as good as the Big Three but quite adequate. Then back to the testing building. Two hours to go. The seats were comfortable and large, and she drew her knees up under the skirt and leaned back. Maybe a nap.

Not to be. All she could think of was the study game. She should have asked the price, but maybe it was in the literature. Anyway, it was none of her business.

Then the wide double door opened, and the test-takers returned. One after the other, and then came Jewelee. Her beautiful hair was scrunched and untidy from running her hands through it. She had pencil lead graphite on her cheek, and her lips were reddened from being chewed.

Weary eyes scanned the seats and Rowenna waved an arm. The exhausted, bedraggled test-taker made her way between the seats. She plopped down beside Rowenna. She sighed deeply as though she could empty her entire body from all oxygen. She looked at Rowenna with tilted head and half-open eyes.

Rowenna could only whisper, "Was it so bad?"

The answer she got was a weary nod. "Worse. I want to leave right now. I don't want to wait for the score."

Rowenna knew a heavy hand was needed now. "We're not leaving. If we came home without your score, your papa would kill you and then kill me for letting you do it. I'm much too young to die. You're staying right here."

She was rewarded by a shrug and, "Or else what?"

Rowenna patted meaningfully on her right hip. "Or I shoot you and leave your body here."

And then the names were called. One by one, they went forward, took their scroll and left without looking at it. They all knew they already had a certificate… this was just the icing on the cake. Jewelee wrung her handkerchief so tightly it was in danger of unraveling into threads. The waiting crowd had thinned out to a sprinkling, and still her name was not called.

Well, someone had to be last, and this time it seemed to be the suffering Jewelee.

"Miss Jewelee Turner."

She managed to balance on her wobbly feet and go forward. The official motioned for Rowenna to come forward as well.

"Miss Turner, sorry to say we were not able to test you thoroughly. Occasionally this happens, but this is the first time it happened for me, and I am so excited for you. We are aware when a score of 100% is earned, that is not a true test of what is known… as we do not know how much farther that person could go."

Rowenna's smile was forming, and her friend's mouth and eyes were opening. "I have to take it again…?"

"No. I have your Certificate right here, and you are qualified to teach tomorrow… even today. However, there is something you might want to do, and I would advise it. For those who score 100%, there is another test in Fayetteville, and we advise you to take it. It will give you an extra advantage in getting a position. There will likely be a dozen or more in this part of the state who will also qualify to meet in two months. That is a test for higher skills, and you should do well. Can you go?"

"NO! I'm through!"

Rowenna grinned widely. "Don't listen to her. I will bring her to Fayetteville, or her papa will kill us both. This is a really big thing with him. This will give him more bragging rights around town."

The official grinned and nodded. "I truly understand, and we will look for you both. Here is what you need to bring."

Rowena accepted the papers and walked away, and the exhausted girl followed. The short January day was fading, and there was just enough light from the street lamps for them to cross the street to the hotel room.

The door to their room closed behind them, and Jewelee announced to the furniture of the room, "I'm not going."

Rowenna just smiled. She'd been up against this attitude before. She'd seen her friend through this bad and worse... happening before each and every test over their eight years of school. Sometimes she laughed at her, sometimes she tried to encourage her, and sometimes she pitied her. This was a time for pity because it should be such a joyous, happy occasion that she had made a perfect score, but Miss Jewelee Turner preferred to stand at the darkening window and stare at the vapor streetlights coming on up and down the streets.

Morning came, and they ate a dreary breakfast, but at least Jewelee was speaking sensibly. Papa now had something he could talk about on the streets. His fourth child and only girl managed to complete her test and would someday be a school teacher. Other than the unofficial mayor, the preacher and the postmaster, the school teacher was about the most admired position in the town. For certain he would make sure he shared her reflected glory, for didn't he... personally... make sure she got down the hill to school every day?

Even when every rock in northwest Arkansas was coated in a casing of clear ice, and every step was to take your life in your hands...? Still, he got her to school. Looking from that point of view, he'd earned the praise... hadn't he?

And by noon, the Frisco had chugged and huffed its way into the depot, swishing a lot of steam as it stopped. Two girls, each with a mind full of thoughts, stepped off onto the platform, and the Frisco was on its way again.

...Huffing, puffing and chugging, trying to get speed enough to make it up Echo Mountain.

*I Kings 18:38
**II Kings 6:6
3*II Kings 2:11
4*I King 17:14
5*II Kings 4:5-7
6*I Kings 17:6
7*II Kings 2:8 and 2:11
8*II Kings 13:20-21

THE WONDERLFUL MEDICAL BOOKS

When Rowenna saw the package, she knew she'd need to take it to Thimbles and Spools and break it apart. How did five books manage to make such a big package and be so heavy? She struggled it that far and opened it. The whole ordeal was of great interest to the aunts.

Within the cardboard packing was:

MIDWIFERY FOR NURSES

MANUEL OF MIDWIFERY

HYGIENE FOR MOTHER AND CHILD

CAUSES AND CURES FOR THE COMMON COLD

INFLUENCE OF ONE DISEASE ON ANOTHER DISEASE

SMALL POX, DIPTHERIA AND SCARLET FEVER

CLEANLINESS IS ALMOST GODLINESS

DISEASES OF THE CHEST

CARE OF THE SICKROOM

BENEFITS OF SLEEP

Noted on the packing slip was a small explanation:

We have included additional books we thought might be of value. It is unusual for an individual to place an order of this size, therefore we felt there was a good reason for these selections and that the additional titles might prove helpful. Fighting illness and furnishing information is our business, and we wish you every success. The management.

Hmmmmm, well… Someone wished her well. She sincerely hoped she could live up to it, and she picked up the top five books and headed for the hilltop house. First she'd stop in and see if Wally was around.

He was. He was happily on the end of a mop, fiercely wielding the handle, attacking the spot where a small jar of mustard had slipped from a small hand and hit the hard floor. He propped the mop against a counter and leaned comfortable against a display... ready to talk.

Nathan had been figuring the monthly balances and looked up as the front door jangled. Who was that... well, for goodness sake... that person walked like Rowenna. Square shoulders, lifted chin and no-nonsense steps. Headed for her cousin. What a picture she made as she disappeared behind the center display and stepped out again in front of the picture window.

He didn't see her nearly as often as he use to, his duties at the WM having been expanded. But he saw her often enough to remember the incidents.

He had just faced the question that puzzles many young men. Just when was it that a girl turned from a tiresome tag-along to a leader... from a nuisance to a necessity...? He watched as she tilted her head upward toward her cousin in such a flattering way. She had an armload of books... whatever for? But that was none of his business.

She set the books on the counter and stepped back, her white shirtwaist glistening in the reflected sunlight and the froth of lace at the neck and forearm laying against her bare skin.

He absently put his pencil on the desk and continued to look. Near the doorway at the back of the market, just stepping into the store, was his father. Amid step, the older man stopped and centered his eyes on his son, a small smile playing among the wrinkles of his face.

He nodded spontaneously. His son had very good taste. He smiled and joked and sometimes teased the girls who came in the market, but, to his pa's knowledge, he had never stared, immobile and transfixed, at a girl before, especially one of the younger ones. Fourteen, maybe... But she carried herself in a determined manner like one at least two years older.

Was this a passing… what would it be called…? Awakening, or maybe a sudden awareness? He'd known this girl from toddlerhood and more recently because of her cousin, but that look… Hmmmmm….

Old Mr. Wilkinson had never seen that look from his son before. Did it mean anything? Too soon to think, of course, but something was happening to his young and handsome pride and joy and sole heir to a thriving business.

Would he wait for her to grow up? The Moffats turned out good youngens, and she was number thirteen, as the whole town knew. Pa'd just hide and watch. Youngens did what they did, and he was surprised his barely nineteen-year-old had not yet shown interest in one particular girl that his pa knew of. It was time, of course, and was there a chance that the Moffat girl would catch up to him…?

The girl laughed at something, turned and picked up her books, waving with one hand in the direction of his son. "Hey, Nathan! Good to see you." And she turned.

Nathan Wilkinson jerked into reality, "Wait, Rowenna. Do you have a minute? I want to show you something."

Hmmm, this could be interesting. Pa found a small duty nearby… close enough to watch.

Nathan met Rowenna and led her to the Lost and Found chest. Opening it, he lifted out a bracelet. A gold chain attached giant blue glass disks, large as a nickel, together. Each of the chain links also held a tiny gold daisy that swung merrily as the bracelet was moved.

The center of each tiny daisy had a set that sparkled like a diamond when it caught the light. Nathan held it up and mentioned nonchalantly, "Some summer person must have dropped it here, because no one has claimed it in six months. When I saw your new skirt, I thought it was the exact color of these beads. What you think…?"

Rowenna's eyes were glued to the bauble. She really was not usually attracted to costume jewelry, or any jewelry, for that matter, but with the newness of the skirt and the exact color match… Hmmmm.

Nathan studied her expression as she lifted the bracelet from his hand. She slipped it on her wrist and lowered her arm against her skirt. The bracelet slid down her arm and flowed around her wrist. She lifted it again to examine it. She looked up at Nathan with a question.

Nathan shrugged and smiled. "I think you should have that, because it matches your skirt so well. That is… if you like it. I noticed an armload of books. Are you planning on studying for a… teaching certificate…?"

Rowenna shook her head. She was tired and needed to get home. "No, I ordered some books on nursing. I decided if I started having to take care of people who were sick, I should find out how to do it." Then she smiled and looked up at Nathan, tilting her head at his height.

"Is the bracelet really for me… or should you keep it a little longer? It looks rather expensive."

"Nope!" Nathan announced with a flourish. "Six months is long enough, and if it was a summer person, she will never remember where she lost it. At six months it became mine, and now it's yours. And I'd better let you get to your studying."

She smiled and turned, and for a second… just an instant… his hand was on her arm. She turned back and smiled again. "Bye, now."

Old Mr. Wilkinson stood and watched while his son remained as a statue and held her in his gaze until the door closed behind her. Then Pa nodded with great satisfaction. *Well done, son. Couldn't'a done better myself.*

And it was time to study. Gone were the pleasant walks around town and the rides on Mustard to check out the woodland. Gone were most of the hot chocolate parties with her cousin at their aunts' house.

Ma examined the bracelet with interest. It had belonged to Nathan, and he could have given it to any girl, but he gave it to Rowenna because he noticed the color of her skirt. What boy absently notices the COLOR of a girl's skirt? Nathan… the cream of the crop where local boys were concerned, but he was older.

Ma commented, "I suspect that whoever lost this really misses it. This had to have been bought for a special outfit or reason. That's

136

the way things go sometimes." And she watched as Rowenna closed the door to her room, drawing herself and the books into seclusion.

Ma looked up. "Dear Lord in heaven, please don't let our little girl get sidetracked until she manages to scratch the itch she seems to have in her head. Can you do that?" If angels made a practice of using their human voices, Rowenna's angel might have assured her, "Don't worry, Ma. I'm on it!"

Ma continued to think. There was that other thing. Jewelee was beautiful. No little mountain girl had the right to be that perfect in every detail. Not that Jewelee seemed to notice it. She was too busy being afraid of her shadow and fearful of not 'measuring up' in her papa's eyes. But that didn't mean that other people didn't notice, boys especially, and when she and Rowenna were together, the difference was highly visible. But Nathan chose her little girl for the gift of the obviously expensive bracelet.

Enough to set a ma to thinking.

Rowenna thought she'd start with *Common Colds and their Cures*. She didn't know there was a cure. Everyone seemed to have their own remedy, and the cold either lasted a week and a half… or ten days!

But that book looked like about what it would take to use up the time before she would take Jewelee to Fayetteville. Fayetteville! Just imagine! About half her siblings were there or had been living there and come home. Big, wonderful town and the test was early, so they would be staying in the hotel for the night and catching the Frisco at 6:00 am the next day.

The trip would be loads of fun, and she would make sure her beautiful blue skirt was ready for the trip, and of course the white shirtwaist the aunts had made to go with it. Crocheted lace collar and cuffs. Also, of course… the bracelet. It was such fun to dress up sometimes.

She wrote another letter.

Dear Management:

I received the wonderful package with the gifts you sent me. I am certain they will be a huge help when I take my test.

I am thankful every day for the wonderful people that God has put on his earth, and your company must have some of the very finest.

Appreciatively yours,

Rowenna Moffat

Wishbone, Arkansas

She sealed it up, being thankful also to the teacher who stressed the importance of letter writing, and that included thank-you letters.

Three days later, Ma chased her out of the house to get a little air. It was a delicious February day. A week ago they had a sleet storm, but it melted in a day, and it was now jacket sleeve weather again.

She caught Granddad at home. Wonderful! He was the world's best listener. "Granddad, I have to tell you what I saw in Bentonville," and she entertained him with a description of the Bible study that could be taught with games. Granddad had responded that, oh, yes, that must be the one described in the flyer over at the WM.

She waited around for Wally to be free, and they changed out the marquee sign. This one was truly one to create thoughtful observance, and she was to think of it many times in the next years.

"Coincidence: When God chooses to remain anonymous."

Together they went to the Thimbles and Spools and were served hot chocolate.

When they parted, Rowenna loading her arms with the remainder of her books and Wally whistling his way in the other direction, Aunt Georgiana was heard to comment, "If it wasn't for hot chocolate, we'd never see that boy."

And Aunt Cecelia countered with, "Yes, and that could be a blessing. I remember how much boys that age can eat. We get off light with just chocolate, the way that cream builds up with just us and our oatmeal to use it."

Two days later, someone did make a trip to Bentonville for that Bible Study Game. It wasn't Rowenna or Wally. It was Granddad, and on the way, he had a lot to think on. It was natural that Wally confided in his cousin what he would not have told Granddad, and if

Rowenna had suggested the game that might be a temporary answer to his aggravation, Wally would likely have dismissed it out of hand.

However, given to Preacher Clemmons to assign to Wally to spearhead among the other young people, it just might work. Wally had a good work ethic… as long as it didn't mean leaving the WM.

Granddad would check it out and see what it was like. He royally approved of the latest marquee. Coincidence was what he had always suspected… not usually an accident.

EDUCATIONAL TESTING SERVICE, FAYETTEVILLE

The day before the Fayetteville test, Rowenna climbed the bluff behind the church property to the Turner Ranch to spend the day. It was going to be a difficult day for Jewelee, no matter what was done, but Rowenna's presence might help a little.

It was actually possible to reach the ranch by wagon road, but one must drive all the way up to the ridge and then back down. Not worth it most of the time.

The Cryer had sounded out the news of the pair and their Fayetteville trip.

CLASSIFIED ADVERTISMENTS

Miss Jewelee Turner has done herself proud in her test for Teacher's Certificate. She weathered the trip to Bentonville, and now she will be going on to Fayetteville to win even higher commendation. Never be concerned, however, for her safety in the big city. She is fully under armed protection both ways. Riding shotgun to her is the Girl with the Gun, so Miss Turner's pa should relax and not drive himself crazy with anxiety.

Both will return, and that is a promise from your reporter at the Cryer, because I am well acquainted with the Girl with the Gun, and only a numbskull would take her on.

139

Jewelee's papa made the trip down to Wishbone mostly by one horse pulling a sled, and that was the way he got the girls to the Frisco Railway Depot. It would be an hour before daylight when the Mail Run came through Wishbone, but it was almost an express and would get them to Fayetteville in time.

An hour down the road, the Frisco served hot tea... very welcome... and Jewelee had permission to eat a cookie. Rowenna would have liked a boiled egg, but that would have meant a teeth brushing, so she settled for a sausage stuffed biscuit.

Rowenna wore, by demand, what she had worn on the first trip, plus the beautiful bracelet. Jewelee was a trifle superstitious. Everything must be exactly the same, because it must have been lucky. She was not to be shaken from the idea of luck, even when Rowenna teased, "You're right. The harder and longer you study, the luckier you get."

The test would cover five hours. Ten to twelve and one to four with an hour for the furnished lunch and no visitors. They were supposed to 'rest and clear their minds'.

That description not only gave Rowenna a chuckle... it almost had her rolling in the floor. To see Jewelee 'resting' and 'clearing her mind' would have been a sight never to be forgotten.

That gave Rowenna at least six hours to amuse herself, and she had decided not to wander away and risk getting lost. Near the testing facility was a library, and what could be better?

At quarter to four she returned. Grading had been conducted as the various sections were completed, so there was only an hour to wait. The exhausted tester was in no better shape than last time, but now it was over. There were a total of thirty-seven testers who had made a perfect score as Jewelee had, and the air was tense with anxiety.

Jewelee was one of the first called. "Jewelee Turner. Graded Excellent. Your score is equal to those with an additional two years of instruction. You are given a certificate with a Gold Seal of Excellence. Great going."

The girl with the ink-smeared nose and tousled hair received the certificate with a sigh of relief while Rowenna stifled the urge to giggle. Fear of testing was very real for some, and that was never understandable to her. Her marks were never as good as Jewelee's, but no matter… one either passed or failed, and worry never tipped the scales either way.

Another night in the furnished dormitory and back to the Frisco Depot. Passengers were shed along the way, leaving empty seats here and there, and a few were picked up. At one little whistle top, five men were brought aboard.

They sprinkled themselves here and there in the available seats, attracting a fair amount of attention as they were dressed quite casually for a train trip, and all were wearing their holstered guns. Unusual but, of course, not forbidden. It was just that being armed on a passenger train seemed so unnecessary.

At one point, a man seated close to the front went forward toward the engine. Now, why would that be? But most passengers paid little attention.

For a half an hour down the road, the locomotive pulled through the cut-away ridges and trestled hollows of northwestern Arkansas without incident. Then one of the men at the front of the car with the girls stood, balanced himself and drew out his revolver. He shouted an announcement.

"You are now experiencing a hold-up. Obey and you will not be hurt. Someone will come to you to collect your money and jewelry. Have it ready. Put it in the hat he carries and say nothing. You will now lean forward with your heads down and stay in that position. Your engineer is being held by three guns, so don't think of trying to pass a signal."

While he talked, Rowenna stared… listened… her thoughts whirling. This must not happen. When he had said lean forward, both girls obeyed, Jewelee hiding her face in the folds of her dress.

Rowenna bent low and looked forward under the row of seats. Empty spaces with no feet or luggage. Space about fifteen inches high under each seat.Easing down to her knees, she gathered her skirt ruffles aside. Head tipped under the empty seat before her, she assessed the possibilities and decided it was doable.

She had a lot of skirt to contend with, and it kept creeping under her knees. That had to stop. Pausing, she gathered a handful of ruffles and stuffed them in her mouth.

The man was still talking. She couldn't see anything and sincerely hoped she was not being watched. Not so. Across the aisle and one row forward, a man with a slightly bowed head was keeping her clearly in sight.

Under one more seat and she looked up into the face of a tiny lady with wrinkles and gray hair and aghast eyes. Small hand with heavy rings covered her open mouth. Rowenna turned her face upward toward her, grinned, winked and put her finger to her lips.

Under the next row she scooted, with three more to go. Man in one of the seats, and he was aware enough to unhook her shirtwaist sleeve from an exposed bolt, nodding knowingly.

Under the next row, and the gunman detected movement. Staring down at her, he demanded, "What are you doing down there?"

Thinking fast, she looked up at him with wide-eyed innocence. "Sir, my bracelet was on the floor." She didn't say which floor. Or when.

The gunman had no sympathy. "Give it to me." And he held out his hand.

Not in a particular hurry, she raised herself up from the floor to the seat and carefully picked off the bracelet and held it out. He grabbed it and turned back to watching the rows of passengers with bowed heads removing coins and rings. His companion was holding his hat for the loot.

As he started to step away from Rowenna, she lifted her skirt carefully and removed her 22mm from her pettislip holster. The man who had unhooked her sleeve and the one across the aisle watched her with sidelong glances and tense lips.

As the gunman moved another step, there he was... back toward her... in direct and open range of her weapon. What to do now? Thoughts... knowing they had only seconds... batted themselves back and forth in her brain. She could so clearly put a shot through the back of his knee and he would spend the rest of his life with a stiff leg.

But she was going to be a nurse, and they did not damage people... did they? Granddad had said one must never shoot to kill… unless it was their own life or death. What would he say about a permanent wound? And she had only seconds… what? WHAT?

She drew in a breath, stiffened her arm and aimed… just above his boot top and at the edge of his pants leg. Now if he didn't move suddenly… shoot! Don't wait! ZING!

The percussion from her shot within the closed car bounced from window to wall to ceiling, gaining sound as though it came from everywhere. She shuddered and caught the seat before her as the gunman screamed, jerked and fell at her feet… his gun sailing out of his hand.

Rowenna pulled her feet up into the seat and aimed the gun down into his face just as the old lady behind her extended a tiny foot encased in a velvet, button-up boot and gave the gunman's weapon a determined kick down the aisle. It slid into the hands of a young fellow hardly out of his teens and brought of grin of triumph to his face.

Grabbing up the gun, he sprinted forward, knocking himself against the man with the hat, causing a shower of coins and jewelry to cascade down on heads. Leaping over the downed gunman, he headed for the engine, followed by two other men.

One little girl stood up in her seat and squealed with appreciative laughter at the show being played out before her eyes. Clapping her hands with glee, she roused a train car of frightened passengers into roars of laughter that would challenge any comedic play.

The man across the aisle who had kept her under surveillance was on his knees flipping the gunman over and binding his hands with his own braided necktie. Leaving him face down, he scurried to the back where another man had relieved the collector of his own gun and had him backed against the exit door. It took another necktie, silk and imported from Italy, to subdue him, and the relieved passengers began to gather the coins and rings scattered everywhere and sort them out to their owners.

The blue-beaded bracelet was still in the gunman's fingers, and Rowenna leaned forward deliberately and removed it. So doing, she wore her best 'so there!' expression. The Bible didn't say anything about not smirking… did it?

Short conference among the men in which they surmised the same thing was happening in the car behind them. The man from across the aisle asked Rowenna if she could handle the two gunmen while they took the two confiscated weapons and checked out the other car.

Seated side by side and tied to the seats with their own belts, she took her place on the empty seat in front of them. Yes, she could manage it, she decided.

Actually, the second car was not yet aware of the situation. Evidently, their turn was going to be next.

With the fellows again in control, Rowenna edged back into her seat beside Jewelee, whose face was still buried in her skirt ruffles. She looked up innocently and asked, "Where have you been? There's been an awful lot of noise, and you missed it."

What could Rowenna say? She just smiled and assured her friend that she would be there next time it happened.

By this time, the locomotive had reached the outskirts of Huntsville, and it seemed appropriate to stop. It was two hours before the clean-up and interviews were accomplished. The five men were taken to the Huntsville lock-up, and the account of the thwarted robbery was teletyped in every direction... even picked up by Wishbone Depot just as the Frisco came chugging in.

Though the message was clear, Papa Turner had already decided his beloved daughter was dead. Shot in a train hold-up. And here he had located and bought a small, downtown cabin that had no farm land. Perfect for his daughter when she became one of the town's school teachers.

Poor Papa, the worrier. It was clear to see where Jewelee got her own phobia.

CLASSIFIED COLUMN

Everyone is invited to the whole town party for Miss Stockard as she hands the schoolhouse key to Miss Jewelee Turner. Bring food and plan to stay all day. Games for everyone.

Miss Turner was protected by armed guard, as before. Did I not promise their safe return? The Girl with the Gun executed a 'kill shot' to the gunman's pants leg and caused a painful burn on the skin of his right leg... a pain that he will not soon forget.

The Girl with the Gun essentially took on the five armed men who boarded the train and averted a robbery of money and jewelry and possibly lives. She was the girl with something no one else had... except the gunmen. She had her Winchester, and it was enough. Though she had the help of several grown men, they voted that she should collect the $100.00 bounty on the head of the gang leader. Of course, we all know it could never have happened this way if Miss Jewelee Turner had not made a perfect score on her first test.

Right on, Miss Turner! We're rooting for your success with the children, and we wave a fond goodbye to Miss Stockard, who taught most of the town how to read. For the latest about town, you can always count on Jadeen Moffat at the Cryer.

It was time for the town party. Old Miss Gertrude Stockard (pronounced Stock Yard by small boys behind her back) would retire. After sixty years of teaching the young of Wishbone, she was actually leaving. She was moving to Bone Breaker Ridge to a cabin on her nephew's land. She would take her cats and her crocheting and live out her years in leisure. She would be well taken care of, as she had earned a whopping pension, $12.00 a month for life.

When asked why she had said nothing about retiring until now, she shrugged her shoulders under her lavender cashmere shawl. She smiled, re-arranging her cheek wrinkles and squenched her eye under their folds of skin. "I had to wait until after Jewelee's test!" Surely anyone would know that.

But they didn't. "What did the test for Jewelee have to do with it?"

She tartly replied, "If you have to ask, you don't know Jewelee. She will be one of the best teachers this school ever had, if she just doesn't have to take another test. In fact, you'll be lucky if Huntsville or Bentonville doesn't sneak her away from you with a better salary." That said, the day-long celebration continued.

Miss Stockard would be missed… for an absolute fact.

So the summer began with Rowenna's nose in the books and Jewelee happily getting ready to take over her class of likely 40 children from grades one to four. Though she melted at the thought of a test, she could hardly wait for the next school term to begin.

Granddad had spent his hour in Bentonville, and he came back with the Bible Study Game. Preacher Clemmons received it with pleasure. Wally was asked to stop by the church when he had a chance.

"I have a project for you if you can manage it. I know you are the best one to handle this wonderful Get to Know Your Bible as a Friend Game. I'd like you to take it and look it over, because with your ability to explain, your attention to detail and knowledge of the young people of Wishbone, I know it would be in good hands with you.

"From what I can see, it would acquaint the game players with content and subjects that never reach the pulpit, and on top of that, I think it will be a lot of fun. There are said to be a dozen different games in here, approaching the subjects from different viewpoints. I'd like you to look it over and get back to me... can you?"

Sixteen-year-old John Wallace Hopkins looked at the colorful cardboard box, and his eyes caught the word 'Study'. He smiled wryly and nodded. He had been caught, and he knew it. He had been warned, so it was no surprise.

He took the box and thanked the preacher. He was smart enough to know one cannot argue with God and win.

But, at least, he was still at the WM. This project would have its own evenings at the church, and it did, actually, look like fun. He walked away and headed up the hill toward home, his mind a whirl of thought.

At least now he knew which way he was going. And somehow, in the back of his mind, he knew this was not the end, but he was, mercifully, going in the right direction. He would be seventeen in one week.

One person who was rapidly attracted to the idea of a weeknight get-together was Jonathan Calhoon, recently having become eighteen. His father had just inherited a bundle of money, and he had bought himself a dream. Half a hillside, it was, that was located on a place that was called Bald Knob and was stretched just south of Dead Horse Springss. It had conveniently come up for sale.

His papa had just created a wide wagon-and-buggy road down to Wishbone and paved it, at great expense, with enough gravel to make it an 'all-weather' road. Young Jonathan considered this as a way of escape out to what was left of civilization. The town of Wishbone.

Papa, an avid hunter, had long dreamed of his own hunting lodge, and now he had the means. Jonathan actually thought it was a good idea… for Papa… and he didn't mind being part of the dream, but now he pined for a spot of social life. He had read with interest the Cryer Classified Advertisements, intrigued by the updates on the Girl with the Gun.

Clever they were, and when he met the author at the church get-together and caught a glimpse of the deep auburn curls and impudently turned up nose, he was smitten. He was determined that his life and Jadeen's would immediately change, and he was half right. First, he must get Jadeen's attention.

There would be a change but not totally immediate. He had yet to meet the mountain folks' reticence at accepting strangers, but young Jonathan was willing to persevere for what he wanted.

Jadeen spoke out by advertising the Thursday Evening Club… as she dubbed it. She also updated the world about her sister.

CLASSIFIED COLUMN

Several wagonloads of gravel needed at the site of the coming Calhoon Hunting Lodge just south of Dead Horse Springss. Leave information with the Wishbone Cryer office.

The Girls with the Gun has pocketed her weapon in favor of medical books. She decided that if she is going to do what she does, she might be able to learn a better way to do it. We wish her luck, and we hardly get a glimpse of her around town anymore.

Spring sale of farming equipment at Marshall's Machine shop. Also rakes, shovels, scythes and what-have-you.

More announcements followed.

Young Jonathan was radiantly surprised to realize the hunting lodge property was a scant half-mile from the outlying edge of the property belonging to the pa of the talented red head of the classifieds. That was going to make things infinitely easier for him.

Jadeen had been totally accurate about the position of her sister's nose, and Ma was forced to intervene. Thirteenth Kid, who was the wandering nature girl, lived in the words of her books. Ma sought reasons to shoo her out, so she could remember that she lived in a world of other people.

Sometimes the 'shoo' was toward household chores, but mostly it was a trip down to Wishbone for this or that... usually from the WM. The heir to the WM, like most young fellows, read the classifieds to keep up with what was going on, and now he could even admit to himself that he scanned first for words about the Girl with the Gun.

Her frequent trips to the market kept him alert. He really was going to say something to her soon... but what? She was almost five years younger, and while that did not mean a great lot now... it had when he was ten and she was five, trying to keep up with Wally at six and a half and doing a rather good job.

When she came for a can of baking soda, even Nathan was convinced that she had been sent there to get her nose from the book for a breath. No one in the mountains ever ran completely out of baking soda.

So when she stepped through the door with her light brown hair ribboned like a little girl... Her smoothly-tanned face sober... but friendly. Her dress of tan with yellow flowers... slightly faded and barely below her knees… how could he possibly look away? He couldn't.

"Rowenna! Just the lady I was hoping to see."

She looked up, somewhat surprised, as though she just looked up from a page of information and he had just stepped into the room. Quick smile. When she smiled… just at him… she sent tickles down his back. Not just tickles because he was a fellow and she wasn't… it was more like tickles of admiration. At great sacrifice to her preferred lifestyle and her habit of roaming free, she was dedicating herself to something that should be considered unattainable by her.

He was very good at reading between the lines of Jadeen's 'updates'. Wally's little cousin, Row, had something that pulled her… where…?

Maybe he could find out how she was handling it, and maybe it would help him in some way. He loved his pa, and the WM had made his life comfortable. He knew Pa was eager to turn it over to him. The thing was, Nathan really didn't want it. That was hard to admit, even to himself.

But pharmacists in small towns were very important. New medicines were discovered daily. He would like to own his own business in Wishbone… small enough for him to operate on his own. He would have the latest medical preparations and other needed items like braces, crutches, even wheelchairs. He knew of times a wheelchair was needed only for a short time, so a small rental would make it affordable. So many dreams… but so far away.

It would take at least a year of study, and that would be all the way down to Little Rock, or maybe Fayetteville would have it. Also money, but that should not be a problem. He was paid a small salary, which he had saved. Pa would help, of course, but getting him past his dreams… that was the problem. He had tried to say something, but Pa just could not conceive of his son not wanting what he wanted so badly to give. So now, what to do…?

Rowenna stepped through the door. Steps sure and steady… not flouncy like so many girls walked. They needn't have bothered, Nathan surmised. Fellows notice girls whether the girls want them to or not. Flounces hardly matter, actually.

Someday he would take Rowenna aside and have serious words. Today just might be the day. He drew in a breath and 'took the bull by the horns,' so to speak. "Rowenna... are you in a hurry today?

Surprised at the question, Rowenna responded, "Uh...."

Bravely, Nathan plunged on. "Because if you aren't, I'd like to take you somewhere for something to drink or...."

Focusing on the unexpected invitation, she offered, "To the Big Three?"

"Well, no. I was thinking of the diner if you had the time."

Rowenna nodded. That told her a lot. He, for some reason, wanted to talk... not just a light chat with Wally's cousin.

Nodding, she told him, "I have time. Ma doesn't want me back for at least an hour."

He'd suspected as much. "Pa... I'm going to be gone for a little while. Wally'll be back anytime."

"That's good, son."

Together they walked down the flagstone sidewalk together, both somewhat tense, sensing a change in relationship. Face to face at the tiny tables of the diner, they decided on cookies and tea. Can't go wrong with cookies and tea, and words are so much easier when food is present.

"Rowenna, I have a question. I want to know how you're getting along. Not like 'Hi, how are you,' but something more. There has been a great change in you this year, and it seems to be getting greater. I really admire your dedication and really want to know what you'd like to have happen... but it isn't any of my business, so I won't ask."

Rowenna nibbled the cookie and searched among possible answers for the best one... the one that he actually wanted. "Well, I...."

He nodded and broke in, "I wondered, because I'm facin' a change, and I know someone is goin' to get hurt, but it's my life. I think your pa and ma may understand children better than mine, bein' just me and my sister. He thinks because he produced me and fed me, I belong to him. Am I making sense?"

She hesitated, and he continued. "I really do know that you're not yet fifteen, but you seem so much older. If I'm making you uncomfortable, we can...."

"NO! I'm just thinking. I've never been asked this before, so I'm trying to understand. But what I remember is one of my Granddad's lessons when he talked about the man who knew he must dock his dog's tail, but he didn't want to hurt him. So he decided to cut off only an inch at a time and let it heal up before he cut off another inch. Granddad told me that if something has to be done and there's no way around it, get it over with so the cut can heal up just once."

Nathan's head tilted with understanding and he grinned an attractive, one-sided grin. "Never heard that before. It makes things really clear."

Rowenna's turn to grin. "Well, you've never had Granddad to explain things and give you answers to questions that haven't happened yet. Fact is, Nathan, Granddad's always around, and he has time. But I think you already know what you want."

"You guess right. I want to be a pharmacist and live right here in Wishbone the rest of my life. But for Pa, it means two things. I would not be taking over the WM, and I would be gone at least a year. That sort of runs against 'Children, obey your parents'."

A nod and a smile. "You did obey when you were a child. Now you're a son but not a child. Sons are advised to 'honor' their parents... if I'm remembering the Bible right."

Nathan slid the last chocolate chip cookie toward her and folded his muscled arms across his chest in a clearly defensive manner. Lips firmly together and square-ish jaw clenched. Nodded slightly. "It'll not be easy."

She took the cookie and picked out a chocolate chip, popping it into her mouth. "I know what you mean. I hated that gunman in the train, and I wanted to shoot him squarely in the back of his knee so he could never walk straight again. I was so mad I trembled and thought I might miss, but I had to do something."

An understanding nod. "You know... I actually wondered about that. Jadeen makes things sound so simple and easy. But you were prepared to shoot, so you did... and now you're preparing for something else. That's what I have to do."

A refill of tea and the conversation passed to lighter subjects. They really found conversation easy, once they got going.

Back at the WM, Nathan turned to her. "Can we do this again? I really enjoyed it."

A smile and a nod were her answer. She picked up the baking soda that Ma didn't need and left. He watched her until she was out of sight. She looked like fourteen but acted at least twenty. Most intriguing, and maybe she gave him the courage he needed.

Nothing much new happened for the next bunch of months. Wally was doing famously as a leader of the study group. Nathan applied for and received a slot for the fall semester at Fayetteville. Jonathan Calhoon managed to occupy as much of Jadeen's time as possible, and Jewelee was on a rosy cloud most of the time.

In due time, Rowenna finished her ten books and had reviewed the paper-clipped parts she had thought might be important. She had requested the test be sent to retired minister Reverend Irvin Hopkins and schoolteacher Miss Jewelee Turner. She now sat at Jewelee's teacher's desk while Granddad and the teacher wandered about.

Rowenna was now sixteen. Jewelee was sixteen and a half, and she had taken command of her class like a wild turkey hen with their massive broods of twenty or more. She was a natural, and it was the top compliment of her short life when Rowenna insisted she administer the test. Seemed appropriate, somehow.

Completed pages of the test were enclosed in the furnished packet and taken by Granddad to the Post Office. Then the test-taker was taken to the diner. Tiny table. Close, face-to-face encounter. Relaxed test-taker.

"No, Granddad. I did my best, and it's gone. If my angels sent me a test too hard, then that was not my problem… was it?" A smile softened her indictment of the angel's guidance, and she took another bite of her pecan pie. The diner made really good pie… especially pecan from the native trees.

"But Granddad, I keep having dreams. Crazy ones that don't make sense. Do you think that's normal?"

"Yes. Not a reason to worry, I would say. When something changes, I feel that you will know it. A lot of people try to make sense of dreams, but I always felt that if they were to mean something to me, then it would be clear enough for me to understand."

"Thanks. I wonder how long it takes to grade my test. I guess I'm not in a hurry, though." Was that actually the truth?

Meanwhile, however, there was Nathan. Walks down to the river when the weather was good. The fun at the Thursday evening study games at the church. Time together began to be cherished, as it was drawing near to being over. He would be gone at the end of summer....

The greatest thing they had in common was the courage it took to break away from the expected. It seemed incredible to the pair that so many words could be said about what was happening separately to each of them.

And the reply came from Memphis. Instead of a letter, it was a box about the size of a flat shoebox. Nathan was with her when she picked it up, and they found a bench while she removed the outer paper. With a degree of apprehension, she lifted the lid.

Inside was a cardboard roll of the kind used to protect rolled documents. She carefully slid out the parchment paper, which unrolled in her hand. She read:

THIS IS TO CERTIFY

That Miss Rowenna Moffat has completed each and every requirement of the Memphis School of Nursing and has comported herself with the dignity required of the profession she seeks. She has proved to be diligent and has acted in a timely manner with all of her assignments. She is hereby deemed qualified by this establishment and ready to act as a nurse of many duties.

Signed: Miss Elizabeth Corning, Principal

Tucked in the box was a letter and a starched white hat of the kind that nurses wear. Beside the cap was a letter.

Dear Miss Moffat,

It is with extreme pleasure that we send you this Certification and the white hat to get you started. We were very interested in your test results, and they were highly adequate and should make you proud.

153

We took the privilege of adding to your score certain points for your initiative, dedication, resourcefulness and determination. All of these are most certainly as important as the knowledge of the course, which can be learned by most students who really try. We had wagers here as to whether you would complete the assignments, and I am glad to say I won.

I hope you will not have to apologize for your age at the beginning, but the gold seal on your Certificate will have meaning for those who will be hiring you. Not everyone earns the Gold.

The nursing profession will be the better for your having decided to join it, and I am certain we will hear more from you through the years. One of our clever instructors remembered reading in the paper of a fourteen-year-old who stopped a train holdup, and the name was the same as yours. We found that very interesting and only hope the Girl with the Gun will be on the train with us when we meet a robber.

So we pray our Heavenly Father sends his angels to watch over you, because the road you have chosen will not be easy.

Yours when you need me,

Miss Elizabeth Corning

Nathan waited until she read it and then asked, "Read it to me, will you?"

He studied her face, and as she read, those same chills of admiration traveled up and down his arms. He would be leaving in mere weeks, and he missed her already.

CRESCENT HOTEL, EUREKA SPRINGS, USA

Two hollows over from Wishbone, a few things were happening. Not big, earth-shakingly new things, but a small new breath was being breathed into some older ones. Interesting things sort of happened under the radar of common view.

The massive stone Crescent Hotel of Eureka Springs had its birth in the early 1800s when Arkansas was popularized as being one of the states that had warm, bubbling mineral water in various places. A city down south was actually named for the hot water. Hot Springs, Arkansas had been used by the first people long before it became a state.

The tiny mountain town of Eureka Springs shared in these heated mineral bubbles that many thought were medicinal. There were those who would attest to their power in easing aching muscles and in improving breathing difficulties. Hence, the construction of the hotel was built mainly from native stone and, in places, had a wall that was more than 16 inches thick.

Then came the Civil War. The history books do not have much to say about that state's role in the 'war of the brothers', but that omission stemmed from the lack of information. Like a lot of other southern/midwestern states, it was covered with a convoluted topography left over from its formative period. Caves aplenty existed, and stones for building were abundant, but information passed more slowly.

So at the Crescent Cave… that was hollowed out of the side of an exceptionally large mountain… was cleaned out, and a building was built around it. It enjoyed an amount of popularity by the rich who could afford to pamper themselves. A spur rail line was scooped from the mountains of southern Missouri for the sole purpose of transporting passengers to the bubbling mineral waters of Eureka Springs.

Then came the war, and its need for hospitals was paramount. Every cavern and cave was called into purpose. The Crescent Cave became the Crescent Hospital and did its duty to the wounded from the war.

After the war, the interest in the hotel died down somewhat, and it was just used for local summer people. Again a summer bathing spa for the rich and famous.

Then Arkansas began to feel the need for medical service of a kind that could not be performed by their few doctors, and the rough terrain made doctors rare in the mountains of northwestern Arkansas.

In the year of 1905, the Crescent Cave/Hotel was again looked at with a nursing college in mind. It had great difficulty getting started because of the roughness of the land and the lack of leaders willing to get something started.

Another difficulty was that the hotel was expensive to maintain, so the fee (loosely referred to as 'tuition') was too great to be afforded by those girls who would be interested in becoming nurses. The school finally dwindled to nothing, but there were a few women with a fierceness of purpose that would not let it die. There had to be a way to train nurses the way it was done in Memphis, Tennessee.

There just had to be a way, and they would find it, even if they had to hack it from the stones of the mountain with their bare hands. So much was said about this revival that it even interested Laverne Moffat... the actress.

She was intensely interested in what was spun off from the interest in the Crescent Hotel to a separate, more affordable building on the edge of town, which they humbly referred to as a 'laying-in hospital'. Sneers from the community festered like grass burrs on the lawn... insisting that no woman with any sense would produce her child anywhere other than in her own cabin... if that was at all possible.

The only trouble with that was that no one asked the women. Forging against public opinion, the ladies who were 'in a family way' flocked to the building that offered relatively painless childbirth and instant, experienced care of the baby. For the first two years, the pleased former patients spread the word. Comfort and reasonable cost brought so much 'business' that more help was needed, and the help would be called 'nurses'.

The next trouble was that nurses required the knowledge that the mountain girls greatly desired but did not have. Especially the intense emphasis on total cleanliness. The amazing survival rate of this hospital was its own advertisement, and the success extended to those babies born at less than full term. So many tiny preemies were saved against all odds.

So a 'school' for nursing was born. Lack of capable administrators and trained teachers hampered progress, and on two important occasions the whole idea was essentially 'aborted'. There were, however, those who still would not let it go.

This struggle of will and determination fascinated Laverne. Reaching her own dream had been difficult, but the dream for these mountain girls was almost impossible to attain. And, in the middle of the night, she thought of her sister. Sitting bolt upright in her bed, she stared at the patches of moonlight on her bedroom floor and made a decision. She would look into this 'school' and see if it might teach what Rowenna so passionately wanted to know.

Rowenna could well afford the fee, as she had spent nothing of the reward money that she thought she should not have received.

It was late July in 1916 that Rowenna's disturbing night dreams had begun. Mostly they were so insignificant she could not remember details. Granddad had told her not to be concerned… yet. So she hadn't. She had mentioned these to Nathan, and together they tossed the idea about. He suggested the medical books might be a cause…? Who knew, anyway, about dreams….

It was on one of these outings with Nathan that she decided to check the Post Office while she was in town. Hmmm, a letter from Laverne. That had never happened before. Nathan encouraged her to read it… it might be important.

Sis:

You have to come over here. There are some determined ladies from a laying-in hospital who have a lot going on. I keep thinking you need to be there, because there might be something going on that you want to know, and I even wonder if they might need to hear some of what you already know. I just keep thinking about it. I decided in the middle of the night to entice you over her to see what's going on, so I can get some sleep!

My love,

Laverne

Rowenna handed the letter to Nathan to read. Lavern's words described her wish very well. Nathan read the letter and handed it back.

"We can go over there the day after tomorrow. I'll tell Pa, but that won't matter. Three weeks from now, I'll be gone anyway. We'll start very early to give you time to see what you want to see, and I can still get you home by dark."

She stared, amazed, as he laid out the plan. "You think I should go immediately?" Was it so easy for him to see her desire when he had such trouble with his own life?

He nodded. "We should have gone yesterday. Can you be ready to go tomorrow instead?"

Rowenna felt her heart begin to pound at the sound of his words. Hard and crisp, they were. Absolutely certain. No wavering about. What could she do but nod yes? They could get ready this afternoon and be in Eureka Springs by 9:30 tomorrow. She'd spend the night at Thimbles and Spools to save time.

"Nothing big, Ma. Laverne just had some things she wanted me to see, and I think I'd like to go. Nathan will take me and wait around to bring me home. I should be back before dark, and I'll stay in town. Don't worry."

Right... tell a mother not to worry!

By 9:00, they were at the top of the ridge headed down into town. She'd go on past the cabin and attend to business and let Laverne sleep. If she worked last night, she would not have gotten to bed before 2:00 am.

A Miss Hollister met her and took her to a Mrs. Cameron. Mrs. Cameron looked at the Certificate of Completion from Memphis and looked up at her... re-read the certificate and asked, "Are you Miss Moffat?"

"Yes, Ma'am, I am."

"Then, I must ask, why are you here? This is a school."

"Ma'am, I thought I might learn something by being in a school with real people and actual patients. I earned the certificate by myself from books recommended by the school. I was tested by the school, and they gave me the certificate. I would like to learn more, and I can pay the fee. I have a place to live here in town."

"But you're only… sixteen…?"

"Sixteen and a half, ma'am. But I can work hard."

Mrs. Cameron frowned, in thought. "Moffat… where have I heard that name?"

"My sister, Laverne, is an actress at the theater. Maybe…."

"No, it's something else. It was in the papers. Maybe in the Cryer." Then her eyes lit up from memory. "Moffat. Jadeen Moffat who keeps us updated on the Girl with the Gun. Stopped a train robbery, she did! Helped catch a man with a price on his head. Would you know her?"

"Ma'am, it's because of the price on his head that I have the fee for the school, and I would really like to try. If I can't make it, then you could send me away. I really want to learn."

"Miss Moffat, you have put me into a patch of questions. There is someone else I need to ask before I give an answer. Can you come back in two days? I'm having a wealth of ideas I need to work out."

"Do you think maybe…?"

"Come back, dear. That's all I can say right now. Remembering Jadeen's words, I'm thinking you helped with a delivery some months ago. Am I right on that?"

"Ma'am, I'm not sure how much help I was, but I was there. Their little girl had the hard red measles and I was…."

Mrs. Cameron stood. "I remember it all, dear. Now I must get busy, but I expect to see you in two days. Remember."

"I could not forget, and thank you so much." She watched as the woman walked away, her starched white dress whispering against itself as she walked. Rolling her Certificate back into its tube, Rowenna turned away. Strange… how she felt. Rather like standing on a precipice with a strong wind behind her back. Excited and uneasy, all mixed together.

Picking up material for sandwiches, they reached Laverne's by noon. Her sister was excited. "You can stay here by the week for as long as you want. We can put in another bed, so I don't wake you when I come home. We can have such fun!"

"But I don't know what they're going to say. I already have a reputation, thanks to Jadeen. Maybe they won't want me."

Laverne, in her best actress voice, was certain. "They will not only take you, they will want you. Mark my word, lady and gentleman. Just mark my word, they will not let you get away."

They did mark her word... all the way home. Another trip in two days and Nathan would be ready with his buggy. Good thing to have this done before he had to leave.

THE MOUTH OF TWO WITNESSES, PSALM 62:11

"No, Ma, they couldn't tell me for sure, but Laverne is certain. I really think I will get to go there. The school has a lot of childbirth business, she said, and I might even learn what I'm doing. And they're sure to use some of the medicines I studied about."

"But you're only sixteen... and Pa...."

"It's a school, Ma. Just a school... and it's so close. And I'll be with Laverne. Pa can come over any time to check on me. I hope he will. Really, if they take me, I'll be in school in the hospital all day, and I can come home on weekends if someone comes after me. I think."

Pa was not happy either, but there seemed to be no good argument.

The next day, she went to see Granddad. She really needed to see him, and he must have a chance to admire the Certificate.

Just last week, she'd had two strange dreams. She had dreamed that two people brought her a package... a large, silver-white box, actually. She could not tell if the people were men or women, and they both carried the box like it was really heavy. They came to her in their long white robes made of something that seemed to shine.

One of them told her the box was important and that it contained something for her. She felt herself reaching out to take the box, but before she could touch it, it began to dissolve in thin air, and the two people faded into nothing as well. She startled awake, and it seemed that she remembered every detail.

Then, the next night, she had dreamed the exact same thing, only when they handed the box to her, she was permitted to take it.

It had seemed heavy when the people held it, but when it was in her hands, it was as light as though it was an empty cardboard container.

"Open it," she was instructed, and she looked on all sides of it. There seemed to be no place to start to open it, and she had no knife to cut through the sides. "How can I open it?" she heard herself say.

"That would be for you to say," the two persons told her, and they began to fade away as they had before. She stood in her dream holding the box, trying to decide how to open it, and it also began to disappear. She was left holding her hands out before her… palms up. She stood looking at her hands until she, also, faded away, and she found herself sitting up in her bed.

The dreams had been last week, and now she was back. Granddad had treated the dreams seriously, and he had told her of the Biblical significance of 'two'.

In the Bible, several important things had happened in pairs. There was Psalm 62:11, where the psalmist said, "God hath spoken once, twice have I heard this… that power belongeth to God." Then there was the other side of it in Job 33:14, where Job said, "God speaketh once, yea, twice, yet man preceiveth it not." Two verses saying God had all power, but humans paid no attention.

But possibly more easily understood were the two angels sent to pronounce doom on Sodom*, the "two men in shining garments" (angels?) sent to Christ's empty tomb**, two spies who were protected by Rehab, 3* and two fleeces put out two times by Gideon to make sure he was in the will of God. 4*

And there were the two dreams of Joseph, telling him he would rule over his brothers 5*, and there were a number of other occasions. But most important of all might be where Jesus said, "It is written in your law that the testimony of two men is true" 6*. Jesus was quoting the old Hebrew law that said essentially the same thing. 7*

Granddad had thought of these incidents and told Rowenna to watch for what came next. So now it appeared that she would have a school where she could study with others and gain the confidence she lacked.

Rowenna was not much encouraged. "But Granddad, I could not open the box, so I am no smarter than before the two dreams."

The old man was not to be deterred. "You will be, my dear. You will be given something to open the box with. It may not be another dream, but you must watch and see."

Meanwhile, two mountains and hollows over to the west, a conversation was going on. Mrs. Cameron was pleading Rowenna's case before Miss Heppinger, the head mistress and the last word on everything.

Mrs. Cameron had just told the head mistress, "We have a chance to get a student who has already passed the test from Memphis school. We must have her."

"No. We do not admit sixteen-year-olds. Rules are rules, and the age is eighteen."

"But her education. And she did it all by herself."

"And how do we know the certificate isn't fake?"

"It has the right signatures and a gold seal."

"Gold seal, huh? Well, what would the other students say?"

"We could admit her and see."

"No. Rules are rules. We can't be admitting every sixteen-year-old who wants to come."

"Right. We could narrow it down to those sixteen-year-olds who can pay the fee and have a certification from Memphis."

Miss Heppinger sniffed and turned away. Mrs. Cameron held her ground.

"We could also add that a sixteen-year-old must also have nursed two patients through the hard measles and assisted in a childbirth without a midwife."

"But what will people say if we take on a girl who shoots a gun?"

Mrs. Cameron shrugged gently. "When they learn who she is, what will they say if we don't?"

Finally, "Alright. We'll try her. If she is disruptive, she goes. We have enough trouble among the 47 other students to allow one to cause trouble."

"Thank you so much." Mrs. Cameron was striding away with firm steps. Even her heavily-starched uniform whispered so firmly that the sound was almost a scream. She was dead certain that the girl would not be charged a fee but would be placed as assistant to the instructor of the beginners. Old Miss Gardner could use the help in Midwifery. Now, all that had to be done was to figure a way to do it.

* Genesis 19:1
** Luke 24:4 and John 20:12
3* Joshua 2:1
4* Judges 6:37-40.
5* Genesis 37:5-11
6* John 8:17
7* Genesis 17:6

EUREKA SPRINGS TRAINING AND LAYING-IN HOSPITAL

Rowenna had hardly cleared the door of the hospital when Mrs. Florence Cameron sent the teletype to Memphis.

"DEAR LIZ stop ROWENNA MOFFAT AT MY DOOR stop UNDERAGE stop."

Eight hours later the response came.

"AUNT FLO stop GRAB HER HOLD HER stop LETTER FOLLOWS stop."

Mrs. Cameron nodded and smiled with satisfaction. She had been certain, and now she was ABSOLUTELY certain she had done the right thing. The letter came three days later.

Dear Auntie Flo,

I was certain she would turn up somewhere, but I didn't think of your town being so close. The girl is a free spirit, and I fear she will not be with you long, because she is so young and has come so far already. One might say that she is on her way somewhere, and you are the important beginning of her journey.

If you can keep her a year or so, she will greatly benefit from the hands-on experience she did not get with us. You

163

have fewer rules than I have, and you will find a way to keep her. For a while.

I venture to say that neither you or I have seen the last of Miss Moffat and her determination. You are doing a good work there and must try not to become too discouraged. Remember, we are on the ground floor of nursing, and someone has to build the ladder to raise the nurses up. It might as well be you and me.

All my love,

Liz

By the time Rowenna was brought back in Nathan Wilkinson's buggy, Mrs. Cameron had already decided what to do about the age. Until the beginning of the next full term, Rowenna would be termed a volunteer helper. A "Blue Cap" she would be called, and be used as an assistant in various places to give her the widest range possible of experience before the next class started the first of the year. All Blue Caps were temporary, just to see if they would fit the program. No supervisor could find fault with that plan for the girl.

It was hardly light when the Wilkinson buggy rattled along the ridge and down the road into Eureka. Nathan reached across the seat for the hand that was jittering with nerves. She sighed and looked at him. Sober. His dark eyes even darker in the dawn light.

They had an hour to kill. The huge, white building was alive with morning activity. There was the day that must be started, the inpatients and the mothers with babies needing to be fed. Errands to be run. A tape measure for when Mrs. Cameron measured Miss Moffat for her white dress.

A strong smell of disinfectant hung in the air as the floors dried from the morning mopping. Steam issued from the pipes as the boilers were in full process of providing hot water for... everything.

Clean... that's what it had to be, and that was one of the greatest expenses of the project and was the area of the most training. It was hard for some minds to believe there were the 'no-see-ems' called germs that must be destroyed with heat and water. No matter... it would be done.

Nathan hitched his horse to the rail in front of a convenient diner that issued an aroma of coffee. Perfect place to wait and let the jitters settle before she went in. Place to say important words. Place to remind himself that she was only fifteen and that he was leaving for a year.

It was a place to face reality. Life was whizzing by, and it seemed to be taking the two of them along with it at a dizzying pace. Would their grip be tight enough to hang on? To hang together…?

Rowenna sipped coffee. She picked at a buttered waffle. "Nathan, it was so good of you to bring me over here again and mess up your whole day."

Careful, Nathan. But he had to say something. "Rowenna, you did not mess up my whole day. You ARE my whole day. I hoped to do something more than stack cans in a grocery store before I left the town. This may be the most important thing I have done all week. Maybe all year."

He waited, and she was silent. He continued, "I told you that it was you who gave me the courage to do what I'm going to do. That was the truth. I may be able to see you at Christmas to see how things go." That was perhaps the understatement of the year. Maybe all his life. So recently she had moved from being Wally's little cousin… to a girl jumping into life with both feet. So exciting.

And then it was 8:00, and they could go in.

She was met with a smile and guided to Mrs. Cameron and her tape measure. Length, girth and shoulder breadth. Then her feet. White shoes and stockings.

"Rowenna, dear, you are going to be taken on temporarily. That is not unusual, and it will let you see and learn more than you would see and learn in a class. The next class starts the first of the year, right after the Christmas break. That will be soon enough for you. We'll see what happens by then.

"Because of your special classification, you get to wear the blue cap, the same as the messengers, though you will not be a messenger except in an emergency. You will begin assisting our Miss Gardner. She has been a midwife for over forty years and knows about all there is to know and has seen likely more than she has wanted to see, but she is the best. It is my opinion you can be a help to her, and you will certainly observe the best in her field. Later, you will assist others. We are extremely glad to have you."

Rowenna was beaming. Her eyes cast here and there, trying to take it all in at once. "Now, where do I pay my fee and buy my clothes?"

"Oh, I failed to tell you. Blue Caps do not pay a fee, they are volunteers, and the first issue of clothing and gear are free. But there is a special thing I must tell you. You may not wear your gun inside this building. That is a rule, except for the guard at the door. Now, listen carefully. You are to be assigned a locker, and I DO NOT WANT TO SEE your gun at any time. The locker is to be kept locked, and only you and I carry a key. I cannot think of a time I would need to use my key, but it is a rule that I have one. What is in the locker is yours, and I have no time to be snooping into lockers. Do we understand each other...?" Mrs. Cameron paused and looked into Rowenna's eyes with her piercing blue ones, magnified by the thick spectacles.

Rowenna nodded. The matron had just answered an important question Rowenna had been afraid to ask. If Mrs. Cameron did not see the gun, then the gun did not exist, as no one else had a key to her locker. The girl sighed with relief. Granddad had given her orders about the gun, and at this point, she seemed undressed without it.

She was dismissed and told to return the following Monday ready for work. She turned and walked away, forcing herself not to run... so excited were her feet. Her head was already floating.

Nathan was waiting beside the gate post of the yard. She wondered, *would he have waited there all day? He must surely be tired.*

He trained his eyes on her face and knew the news was good. She was fairly bursting with excitement. She stepped past the guard and through the gate, and he resisted the urge to grab her waist and swing her around. His hands so well remembered the feel of her... when lifting her down from the tree.

She leaned toward him and whispered, "I'm in!" Whispered as though it had to be a secret, and if spoken out loud, it might disappear. "I come back Monday."

Back in the convenient diner, she announced, "Everything in that building is white. All except my cap... it will be blue until I can start a real class after Christmas."

"Blue...?"

A quick nod. "Because I will be running errands and helping when I can. First I get to help the midwife teacher." Ducking her head with a sly grin, "I might get to see what I should have done for Emily Parnell. And didn't."

"And you're happy about all of this. It is really what you wanted?"

"Now you sound like Ma. She can't believe what she produced for numbers eleven, twelve and thirteen. Can we stop and see Laverne? She's bound to be awake by now."

One look from Laverne toward her sister, and Rowenna was enveloped in a sisterly hug... one that would never have happened had it not been for the measles and their forced closeness. "I knew! I just knew it was for you. Now you can move in with me, and you only have three blocks to go to get to work."

Rowenna shook her head. "I can't. I live there during the week. I can have four hours free on Monday from 4:00 to 8:00. I have to be checked in by 9:00 pm, or they come looking for me. I have to tell them where I'm going. I thought Monday was a good time to be off, because you don't usually work on Mondays... I thought."

From Nathan. "You have to tell them where you're going?"

A nod. "They say I belong to them, and they are responsible for me. That the rule is for my own safety."

A nod of agreement from Laverne. "Good. I like that. You're only sixteen."

"But you came over here at seventeen."

"Yes, and that is why I know."

Then Rowenna. "Mrs. Cameron says I'll be so tired that I'll be glad to 'hit the hay' by 7:00 pm."

Then they were back in the buggy, climbing the road to the ridge. They faced the west with the August afternoon sun shining through the isinglass windshield of the buggy. It sparkled on the glossy back of the horse and the silver trappings of the harness.

Just before they reached the lip of the hollow, a cloud passed and dimmed the light in the buggy. About three seconds later, it popped out in all its streaming glory, only to dip back again. Rowenna knew, without a doubt in her mind, it was a signal from her angel... and there it was again, just an instant of brightness, before they turned onto the Ridge Road. Twice. The angel message came two times.

In a small way, she would like to have told Nathan, but she couldn't. The encounter with the angel was hers alone, and she was not ready to share, even to the person who had been so good to her. Maybe later.

It was on Ridge Road that he reached for hand, and not because it was jittery. She was as calm as a cucumber in the garden, or perhaps the tortoise that nibbled the cucumbers. All sorts of comparisons slipped through her mind. Seven dishes of ice cream before her, and she could only eat one. Twenty-seven new storybooks, and she was going to be working ten hours a day with no time to read. Five horses like Mustard saddled for a ride, and she could ride only one. There was one comparison, however, that she could share with Nathan.

"Do you have any idea how I feel right now...."

"No, but maybe you can tell me." He turned to look at her... full in the face, his dark, dark eyes glistening with interest.

"I feel like I'm in a flower garden as big as Pa's horse pasture, and it is totally full of flowers... and I have only a small basket to gather them in." She grinned. "Does that sound rather silly or strange?"

"No. It sounds like it came from a girl with a very colorful mind. Perhaps your basket is bigger than you think."

Months later, Nathan was to remember this conversation and see Rowenna standing in the field of flowers, more times than he would ever have thought. Years later, it was as bright an image as it was now in his mind.

And Rowenna was to remember this conversation as her duties grew and her basket seemed to grow along with them. Not everything she dealt with was flowers... but there were enough. More flowers than thorns... actually.

Rowenna climbed to the hilltop house with a full mind. She feared this meeting was not going to be particularly easy. She was right. Ma and Pa tried to be happy for her, possibly with the secret hope that things would not go so well as she hoped. But still, what could they have expected?

Jadeen was overjoyed. Rowenna could see the wheels of her sister's agile mind forming the notice for the classifieds.

The aunts had great difficulty understanding. "But you took the test and passed, didn't you...?"

She tried to reassure them. "But that just meant that now I could go to work." It still didn't make sense, but nothing about this thirteenth kid had made sense. Maybe they'd understand later.

Then Granddad. He was at home. Somehow he must have known.

"Oh, Granddad, I'm so happy. I found out what was in the white box the angels brought me."

"You... found...?"

"I did! I didn't see it until I walked out of the building to come home, but that hospital is huge and white... four stories high. Everything in it is white so it will show the dirt that needs to be washed away. The desks and beds and tables and chairs. Even the clothes. I will wear a white dress and white shoes. No wonder the big box that looked so heavy was white."

Granddad had nothing to say in the midst of this happiness, even though it was taking away a rare pleasure of his life. She was leaving the nest.

"Granddad, the angels said I had to open the box, but I didn't see how I could. But I had help. Nathan and Laverne helped, but my Certificate was the key that opened the lock. I don't think I would have been taken in without the Certificate."

"But you HAD the Certificate. Remember the marquee that said, 'Coincidence is where God decides to be anonymous'?"

And it was Monday. Nathan again traveled the ridge road toward Eureka Springs with Wally's little cousin. It was a goodbye. He would be gone when she came home for a weekend.

He walked with her to the gate and watched as she continued on toward the huge, white building with the rows of windows, polished and shining in the morning sun. He waited as she paused at the door, turned and waved, and then was enveloped within the white box.

He returned to the buggy and climbed to the ridge road. Tomorrow, Papa would take him to the Frisco Depot in Wishbone, and he would also be enveloped within his own future.

"A man's gift maketh room for him and bringeth him before great men" (Proverbs 18:16).

Also....

Thirteen is an unlucky number only if you are on the wrong side. Remember Joshua circling Jericho... once a day for six days... seven times on the seventh day. 6+7=13, and the walls fell!

- BONUS EXCERPT -

SISTERS
ARE FOREVER

1

Seven-year-old Carl Morgan Junior picked up the shiny double-bladed ax and swung it at the base of a persimmon sapling. The limber tree trunk quivered from the blow but stood fast, so Junior swung again.

Six-year-old Freddie Morgan watched respectfully then suggested hopefully, "You get that'n cut down I getta cut the next'n."

"No, you ain't. Six years old, that'd be not old enough to be handlin' a ax. You'd most likely chop off a foot," Junior pointed out.

"Aw, them's the words Pa said to you and you went and took the ax 'hind his back. Iffen you don't let me cut down a tree, I'm gonna tell on you."

"Now, Freddie, you know Pa said them words to me when I was six, like you. But now I got to be seven. They's a lot'a difference 'tween six and seven."

Junior took another swing. The ax blade glanced off the springy tree and struck a flint stone. Sparks flew.

"Wow!" exclaimed Freddie. "Georgie, you and Stanley see that?"

Five-year-old Stanley, and Georgie, who had just turned four, nodded, wide-eyed.

Junior paused, basking in their admiration. "I just done that for the little 'ens to see."

"You gonna do it again?" Georgie wondered, hopefully.

"Reckon not. I gotta be cuttin' down this here tree," their brother explained.

Junior shouldered the ax and again aimed it at the base of the tree. The blow almost severed the small trunk.

"Freddie, you get a holt onto that'n and twist it off. I gotta be cuttin' another'n. Pa gonna be back askin' where at his ax is."

"I won't tell," Freddie promised.

"Likely you'd not have to, him havin' ears to hear me choppin' with it. Freddie, count them logs we got done a'ready. We most likely got logs enough for the floor."

"Let me count 'em," offered Georgie.

"Aw, you can't even count. Get out'a my way."

"Can, too, count. One, three, eleventeen...."

"That ain't right. Now get back," Freddie demanded. "I been to school and you ain't."

Georgie obediently stepped back, pulling Stanley with him.

"We got thirteen of 'em, Junior. That'd be near what you allowed we'd need?"

"Yep. Now Georgie, you and Stanley don't be touchin' this here ax where I lay it down. You'd hurt yourself for shore. Freddie, you drag them logs over to the tree and hand 'em up. Georgie, you can bring along that rope."

Junior Morgan caught the lowest limb of a massive oak and, wrapping his legs around it, pulled himself into the tree. The second limb, a good eight feet off the ground, grew straight out from the trunk of the tree and made a branch with a level fork. A perfect site for a treehouse.

"Hand me up that little'n first and the rope. I gotta tie the first'n down real solid."

Freddie took the rope from Georgie and draped it over the end of the smallest tree trunk. The two younger brothers watched, wide eyed, as Freddie carefully raised the stick and the rope to Junior, who was straddling the limb above. The three boys on the ground watched closely as their brother tied the first floorboard of their treehouse to the limb of the tree.

"I wanna come on up there," Freddie announced.

"You can't. Them little boys ain't big enough to reach them poles up to me."

Georgie took his thumb out of his mouth. "Can I come on up?"

"No, 'cause we'd be havin' to quit work to help you and we ain't got the time."

Freddie handed another small log to his brother who carefully fitted it into place. To make it lay better, he knocked off a few excess chips, which fell down on his brothers.

"Georgie, you pull Stanley back away. Iffen he'd get a hunk'a bark in his eye, he'd go bellerin' to Ma and she'd make us stop."

"Why?" asked Georgie.

"I ain't never figured it out why but that's what a ma always does. Ain't no matter what's bein' done, ya always gotta quit when a little'n gets hisself hurt."

"We ain't got but two logs left," reported Freddie.

"Two's all we gonna need. Hand 'em up."

By now, the ground crew had completely lost sight of the floor builder, due to the six-by-eight-foot platform of small logs covering the limb.

"I'm gonna come on up, now," Freddie announced.

"Come on."

"Me, too."

"Me, too."

"Freddie, you wait down there and boost the little 'ens, and I'll catch their hands and pull 'em on up"

"Me, first," Georgie insisted.

"First," echoed Stanley.

"No, me first," Georgie yelled and shoved Stanley backward.

A stern voice came from above. "Cut that out, Georgie. You gonna have him yellin' and Ma gonna be runnin' out here for shore."

"But I said 'me first' first."

"Yeah, you did," Junior agreed. "Hand 'im up, Freddie."

Freddie grabbed Georgie around the waist but couldn't lift him up to the first limb.

"I know what, Freddie. You come on up here and I can push him up to you."

Whereupon Freddie and Junior changed places.

From his place on the ground, Junior now instructed, "Listen, Georgie, you hold out your leg so as you can catch onto that limb.

Freddie ain't gonna be holdin' onto you for very long, you bein' so heavy."

With a grasp and a jerk, Junior boosted Georgie upward. Freddie grabbed Georgie's upraised hands and pulled. Georgie's leg wrapped around the limb like a possum tail over the henhouse door.

"You got a good holt?" Junior asked.

"Yep," came the answer, as Georgie climbed on up to the second limb and crawled out to the platform.

"Me! Me!" squealed Stanley.

After sizing Stanley's height against the height of the first limb, Junior made a stirrup for Stanley's foot and Freddie reached down, but Stanley didn't catch the limb with his free leg.

Freddie's grip slipped and the small boy dropped back down into Junior's arms.

With a stern voice, Junior refined his instructions. "You gotta help out, Stanley. Freddie can't be holdin' on to you all day. Now, you seen how Georgie done it so you know what you gotta do. Here we go, again."

Junior hoisted Stanley up again and Freddie reached down. Stanley raised his leg but failed to catch the limb. Down he came in a pile on the ground, yelling with indignation.

"Don't you be cryin', Stanley," threatened Junior. "Ma'll hear and then we gotta go in."

Stanley whimpered and pouted his lower lip. "Me, first, too," he pled.

"What we gonna do?" wondered Freddie, turning to Junior for the answer.

Junior looked around, sighing wearily. His eyes rested on a small wagon used for light, one-horse hauling. The wooden box of the bed was tight for hauling grain, and it stood about three feet off the ground.

Junior's practiced eye determined it to be about the right height.

"Freddie, come help me get that cart over here and he can climb up on it. Then it'd be easy for us to get him on the rest'a the way."

As instructed, Freddie jumped down. Georgie yelled, "Me, too. I gotta help."

A quick response came from his brother. "No, you ain't. It was trouble enough gettin' you up there," Freddie pointed out, so Georgie now had permission to settle back to enjoy the show.

The three brothers walked up the incline toward the waiting cart.

"Ride?" suggested Stanley, hopefully.

A quick decision and Junior answered, "Yeah, get on in it. Won't be no heavier with you in there, once we get it to rollin'."

The two bigger boys leaned against the endgate of the wagon but the ends of the double-pole tongue just dug themselves into the soft ground.

"Freddie, you go around and lift them tongues whilst I shove on it. Bein' downhill, likely it'll go easy once it gets goin'. I'll break it loose, and when it gets to rollin', you just swing them ends on around the side of the tree and drop the tongues to stop it a'rollin'. Ready?"

"Ready," Freddie answered, as he positioned himself between the poles and lifted them.

Junior applied his shoulder to the endgate, dug in his heels and the wagon began to roll. Freddie ran to keep ahead of the wheels, holding tight onto the bouncing tongue poles.

"Go to the tree," shouted Junior.

"I can't!" yelled Freddie. "It's tryin' to run over me!"

The cart rumbled down the incline and passed under the treehouse platform, then headed for the bluff overlooking the Tuscalara River. Junior's mind accurately projected the certain outcome.

In wide-eyed horror, he gasped and shouted above the gleeful and excited laughter of Stanley and Georgie. His command was somewhat muffled by his brothers' excitement.

"Drop 'em, Freddie! Drop 'em!"

"Huh? I can't hear you."

A few decibels louder, he repeated, "Drop 'em! Let 'em fall down!"

The cart was now nearly fifty feet from the overhanging bluff of the pasture. Junior ran ahead to help turn the cart away from the river, continuing to shout, "Drop 'em, Freddie! Drop 'em! You hear me?"

"Yeah, but I can't. It's tryin' to run over me."

"Drop 'em, anyway!"

At this moment the right front wheel of the cart struck against a large rock, spinning the cart completely around. Freddie was sprawled onto the grass by the tongue poles, skidding on his chin and elbows.

The cart proceeded merrily on toward the bluff, endgate first. Junior reached the speeding wagon and barely touched the tongue pole before it bounced out of reach.

Stanley crouched down into the corner of the cart, clutching its sideboards screaming, "Mama! Mama!"

In desperation, Junior screamed, "Come on, Freddie. We gotta catch it!"

Freddie, green from the grass stain and red from blood streaming from a cut lip, obediently jumped up and ran after Junior.

At the very edge of the bluff, the wagon bumped against a tuft of grass and hesitated for a moment, then it sailed out and over the fast flowing river. It seemed to hang motionless in the air before settling downward, the tongue shafts whirling.

Stanley's terrified scream carried out over the water and seemed to echo against the opposite mountain.

Junior, white as chalk, and Freddie, a mixture of red and green, watched the wagon settle onto the swirling water of the fast-moving river.

It spun around, righted itself, then headed downstream. Stanley's terrified screams became faint and indistinct as the wagon disappeared around the bend of the river.

2

Lorena Morgan closed the cabin door softly and walked toward the bluff to her own private thinking place. Two-year-old Jamie would sleep for at least two hours and she really needed this time alone, this being the first moment that she knew, absolutely for certain, that she would bear another child. Yesterday she thought so, and today she was sure, for hadn't she been at this stage five times before?

There was even a name for the feeling. It was the quickening. It was that moment, just an instant, really, that a woman felt herself projected into the future. It was the feeling of being part of all mankind. It was that delicious wave of elation at the beginning of the creation of a new life.

Except that this moment brought her no elation.

This first, uplifting wave was followed by the rock hard impact of knowledge that this child within her did not belong to her. The wonderful miracle of a baby growing under her heart had nothing to do with her. The child was not hers now, nor would it ever be.

Slowly she sat down on the rock ledge, drawing her feet under her skirt. The rock was massive and sloping, offering a perfect view of the miniature silver bridge over the restless river, a tiny, green-pastured farm or two, and the distant slope of Five-Mile-Hill.

The bluff also overlooked the Tuscalara River with its racing, swirling water and often it seemed to relieve her anxieties and weariness, just by the sight of it. Its currents and movements were alive and restless, yet orderly and contained. The river entered her life from somewhere to the east and disappeared just around the bend in the west, but for a moment, it passed before her and it was hers. As it passed her bluff, it was her river, and she was content to sit and watch it flow.

She was sitting there on the ledge watching the river and the sky above, hoping for its peace to settle onto her, when she heard Stanley's screams.

"MAMA! MAAAMMAAA!"

She turned instinctively toward the sound and saw, in bold relief against the blue sky, a square shape similar to a small wagon. The strange shape hung in the sky for an instant, then began to settle onto the water. From this shape came more screams.

Lorena watched, fascinated at the illusions a mind can create. Then she walked to the edge of the bluff for a closer look. She saw the shape swirl around on the water and rapidly head downstream, bearing the outline of a small boy clinging to its sideboards.

"MAMA! MAMA!" came the hoarse sound, piercing her illusion in a most unnatural way. Then realization clutched at her heart. This was no illusion! She gasped and ran back to the cabin, to the bed of the still sleeping Jamie. What now? Where was Carl? She turned this way and that, but it was as though her feet were glued to the floor. *Think, Lorena,* she demanded.

As a reflex action, she grabbed Jamie into her arms, hugging him. His sleeping head lolled over on her shoulder, his black lashes heavy against his rosy cheek.

She put him back on the bed where he sighed, turned over and continued to sleep. She tapped her chest with her fists, seeming to try to keep her beating heart from stopping.

3

Junior and Freddie watched the wagon sail into the air and splash down into the water. They turned, as one, and ran to the calf shed in the lower pasture.

"Pa! Pa!"

"What you boys doin' down here?"

"Pa, you gotta...."

With fatherly concern, Carl began with what was the most obvious problem. "Freddie, what you done to your face? Here, we gotta clean you up. Junior, something punch him in the mouth?"

"No, Pa. You gotta get Stanley. We...."

"Now, Junior, I told you and Freddie to quit sneaking off a the others just 'cause they're littler. I told you...."

"Pa, listen at me! Stanley got in that little wagon. You gotta come...."

"Now, Junior, I got work to do. You boys ought'a be able to get him out. Freddie, what did you do to your chin?"

With eyes wide and frightened, Freddie shook his head vigorously, "No, Pa. You got no time to be talkin' at me...."

Seeing they finally had their father's attention, Junior plunged in again.

"Yeah, Pa. Freddie's sayin' the truth. Stanley got in the little wagon and it rolled over the bluff!"

"Bluff? The wagon? Stanley? Good Lord a' Mercy!" Carl stuck his head out of the shed and yelled, "Marcel, come help me get Stanley out'a the river!"

"The what?" came the unbelieving response.

"Grab a couple's horses and run!"

Marcel McCann, brother-in-law to Carl, was fence-mending along the bottom calf pasture. Being no stranger to emergencies, he dropped his tools and jumped onto the nearest mare. "Come on, Buck," he yelled to the white pony nearby, and the pony came trotting after the mare.

"What you needin' with the horses, Carl?"

"Stanley rolled into the river in the little wagon. Gotta get 'im!"

Carl paused from running long enough to swing onto the white pony as it came galloping past him, directing the animal onward with a slap on the rump. Guided by a hand on his mane and knee pressure on his neck, the pony ran for the road. The mare and Marcel came lumbering after.

"How far did he go?" Marcel called.

"Don't know," was Carl's answer. "Somewhere 'afore the Mississippi, I'm hopin'. Figure that sharp turn there in town could ground 'im. It'll either stop 'im or...anyway, that's where I figure he'll be."

The pony and the mare galloped down the steep bluff road onto Dogwood Valley Road. From there they clomped across the silver bridge. They stretched flat out as they tore down Main Street where a small group of people, attracted by the screams, stood by the bank of the river.

"They's a kid in the river! A little'n. I seen 'em goin' past like he was a little Noah in his ark."

"Who is he? Why, he's just a little fella!"

"Could get lucky. Looks like the bend'll stopped 'im. Got 'im stuck in the sand bar."

"Preacher's a'swimmin' out after 'em, now."

"Ain't no end'a the surprises that come down that river."

- END OF EXCERPT -

ADDITIONAL BOOK SERIES BY JOANN KLUSMEYER

The Great I Am Bible Story Series for Kids
6 books

The Young Pioneers Adventure Series for Kids
5 books

The Wentworth Triplets Mystery Series for Young Teens
3 books

Footsteps in the Canyon Adventure Series for Young Teens
4 books

Burnt Tree Junction Historical Fiction Series for Adults
6 books

Ozark Mountains Historical Fiction Series for Adults
7 books

Taming the Wilderness Historical Fiction Series for Adults
4 books

The Sheltering Stones Historical Fiction Series for Adults
5 books

The Trilogy of Wishbone Hollow Historicial Fiction Series for Adults
3 books